Student Bodies

STUDENT BODIES
T.T. Madden

This is a work of fiction. Any resemblance to actual persons or events, living or dead, is purely coincidental. The nausea you may incur, however, is real.

Cover illustration and interior formatting by Chris Krawczyk. Edited by philip rowan.

First Edition Published by Little Ghosts Books, July 2025.

ISBN 978-1-7389097-9-7 (Paperback)

Student Bodies

T. T. Madden

Content Warnings:

This book contains depictions of suicidal ideation, self-harm, religious trauma, gender dysphoria, and animal attacks, as well as mentions of on-campus assault.

Little Ghosts Books
Toronto, ON Canada

If you've picked this book up, I hope it gives you
the strength to do the scary thing.

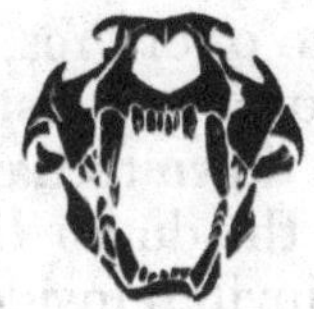

He calls himself Joseph Idlu only because that is the identity of this current face. His real name, the one he was born with eons ago, has long since been declared blasphemy. He quite literally cannot even speak it aloud anymore. Is forbidden from doing so. When he tries to open his mouth to utter it, there is nothing but a void, a hot breath of air, ancient magics preventing him from speaking the required syllables, from even writing them down. He's tried, on multiple occasions, to write his name in the various tongues of men, but every time his hand becomes jittery, and he forgets his intentions, coming away with only a jagged, nonsensical line composed of no letters or characters at all.

Godsdamn the Lupanar. Stupid unholy flesh-priests acting no better than the man-priests do down here. What is the point in being a flesh worshiper if you weren't going to actually enjoy everything the flesh had to offer? The way the priests act, doling out their scripture from their flesh-and-bone towers in the Gancanagh, it's like they've never actually felt the warmth of a cunt, never lapped up a pool of blood, never felt skin under their squeezing fingers, meat between their teeth. What is the point in coming down from on high if it wasn't to enjoy all the little things these meat-creatures had to offer? Yes, he knows some of the Lupanar come down to satisfy their own needs and curiosities, drop down to Earth, interpreted as angels or demons by the dumb, little, mud-crawling things on this rock, invited inside.

He's certain that he and the other members of the Lupanar are the source of some of the human legends of incubi and succubi. Vampires. The dark, hungry things that, with oily-smooth voices, ask to be let inside. He does know for a fact that centuries ago, a young one of their kind influenced a Croatian named Jure Grando, who rose from the dead to terrorize his village in the night. And before that Peter Stumpp, a man they called a werewolf, was gifted the power of the Lupanar to fulfill his dark desires. One of them bonded with Cassilda Karnstein, Queen of Wisborg, who ruled her country as a shadowy vampire. The Lupanar, like those mythical creatures, feast on the energy of humans, but not out of necessity. They are not predators, but connoisseurs, delighters in every available physical sensation.   Thousands of years of their kind interacting with the humans, and yet his one little spree of self-indulgence brought about a punishment that the Lupanar hadn't doled out for millennia—a desecration of his name and a banishment from their realm, Gancanagh.

As Joseph Idlu, he'd killed fifty-two people. Yes, that was more than Jure Grando or Peter Stumpp or any Lupanar-influenced human since. But the number gives him a sense of pride because of where he committed it; America. He's certain he must hold some kind of record here, this kingdom that exists as a monument to flesh, yet also built upon its desecration. The home of the serial killer.

He doesn't know how long it's been since he's been out in the world—since he's really been free—only that it's been too long. Not since he'd taken the body of Joseph Idlu for a spin. Fifty-two deaths in the span of a couple months. A final bow from the seat of an electric chair, and a last little bit of orgasmic throbbing as the switch had been pulled; he delighted in the knowledge that this would not be enough to truly kill him. He'd watched, separate from his own flesh, as the officials in Texas—instead of burying him in an unmarked grave on the property of Anderson Prison, like they were supposed to—fed his body to the pigs on the warden's farm.

Oh, how he wishes he could have been inside the body for that. How he wishes he could have felt the bloodletting knives against Idlu's flesh, the mud as the corpse was thrown into the sty, the feel of the pigs' teeth biting into him, the warmth as his flesh slid down dozens of different gullets, the bubbling stomach acid, the shuttering of sphincters as he exited. He would've been able to feel what it was like inside them, being chewed up and digested. Such a visceral death was one of the few earthly delights he had not yet had the pleasure of experiencing and, to be honest, he didn't even think about it as a sensation he'd like to enjoy until he watched them discard his body. He put it on the list.

The lifetime of a creature such as he and the other members of the Lupanar cannot be measured on the same scale as these humans, and yet the being now using the name Joseph Idlu is determined to make the most out of every moment he is able.

And that must begin with finding a new flesh.

Chapter 1

Frankie Starling stands shivering on the edge of the roof of the Robert Mayer Library, overlooking the snow-blanketed campus of Holstenwall College. Far, far below her, a bronze statue of the school's mascot—a scholarly knight, book in one hand, sword in the other—stands resolute against the winter chill. Frankie pulls her cell phone out of her pocket, marveling that she still has it after everything that's happened, and dials the only number she can think of: Victoria, her roommate.

The phone rings and rings and Frankie wonders if Vic will sleep through it, before her thoughts drift to her mother and father. Children—for that's what she still feels like she is, emotionally, if not legally—would normally call their parents in such situations, after something catastrophic has happened, but Frankie cannot involve them in this. She moved halfway across the country to this school to get away from her parents, from their church, from the place where she felt constantly smothered by images of Christ looking down upon her, judging her. But who will she call if Vic doesn't answer? What will she do if she's left up on this roof all alone? What will happ—

"Egh?" Vic answers, half a word, half a grumble.

"Victoria!?" Frankie asks, trying and utterly failing to keep herself calm. She can feel herself shivering and not because of the cold. Far below, she sees the statue of the knight, and its stillness, its surety, seems to mock her.

"Frankie?" Vic asks, coming to life. "What time is it? Are you alright?"

"Vic?" Frankie can hear the choked cry in her own voice. "Vic, I need you. I've done...I did something bad."

Frankie can hear Vic on the other end of the line asking what's wrong, asking where she is, saying don't move stay right where you are I'm coming to get you, but her words are drowned out by Frankie's own scream, a scream that itself is drowned out by the cold, sharp winds whipping through the air above the campus.

Below her, the night remains impassive.

Frankie lays in her bed in her dorm room, blankets pulled up to her chin. She's curled herself into the fetal position, backed herself into the corner where the walls meet, eyes facing out into the room. Their dorm looks much like everyone else's; only so much you can do with 230 square feet. Aside from the bed which she fell into when she came back, Frankie's side of the room is immaculate. Her schoolbooks are piled neatly onto her desk, plastic bins full of clothes slid under her bed. Soft string lights and inspirational photographs decorate her one-and-a-half walls. A small crucifix she now mildly regrets is the only significant item from her bedroom at home. It hangs just above her pillow, looking down on her.

Frankie can feel its eyes.

Vic's side of the room isn't messy, but it's not as tidy as Frankie's. Some of her socks have missed her laundry hamper and her books and binders are still open haphazardly on her desk. A couple posters grace her walls, actually framed: Vic's favorite band, Darrow Foroi; and some stylized art for old black-and-white horror movies, blessedly free of blood or gore, instead depicting Gothic cities or looming shadows. Frankie told herself they weren't openly inviting any kind of devilry, but it was hard to shake off something you'd been taught all your life. Vic's bed is cluttered with books and clothes, leaving just enough room for her to lie down, but she's not there at the moment.

Victoria Wilson—Vic to everyone else—told Frankie to hold tight, that she'd be back with food, and she was good on her word. Frankie doesn't know how long she's been waiting there curled up in her bed, but the door opens and Vic comes shuffling in with a plastic bag of meal hall food in her hands, brushing the hood of her jacket off her head, shaking off a fine layer of snowflakes.

"Hey, honey." Frankie's heart does a familiar double-take; blooms and then immediately wilts. It's an affectionate word from Vic, the way female friends refer to one another, Frankie has come to understand. But such affectations are still lodged in her brain as something only ever meant to go in one direction, from one gender to another—because she was always taught there were only two—from one romantic love to another. A husband to his wife and back again.

Sometimes Frankie can't believe there's so much about the world she's never heard about until now. But that's what happens when you grow up where Frankie has grown up, around the kind of people Frankie has grown up around, beneath the eyes of a monolithic entity that teaches you nothing but its own propaganda.

Vic normally wears a lot of makeup, but this morning she's bare, her eyes unshadowed, her lips undarkened, hair tucked underneath a wool cap. In or out of makeup, Frankie has always found Vic a lovely girl, and at that thought she winces again, her brain immediately wandering back in the direction of wondering what her mother would think should she hear a thought like that. It wasn't dangerous on its face, she'd say, appreciating the God-given beauty of your friends, but deviancy was a slippery slope. Like with Vic calling her honey. Such thoughts were the devil whispering in her ear, her mother would say.

Vic pulls her coat off and steps out of her boots, and Frankie feels the need to avert her eyes from Vic's tank top and bralessness, from her sweatpants with their rolled-up waistband, Vic's belly peeking out from under her askew shirt and her hardened nipples visible. The little voice in Frankie's head that sounds like her mother tells her Eyes straight ahead.

"I didn't know what you'd want," Vic says, sitting down on Frankie's bed and plopping the plastic bag between them, "so I just got a little bit of everything." Vic whips her hat off and tousles her long, dark hair. She begins popping open to-go containers, revealing pancakes, waffles, bacon, eggs, the sweet smell of syrup and butter. Vic pulls out lidded cups of orange juice and coffee, handfuls of individual sugar packets and half-and-half containers, spreading the massive feast out across the bed before

Frankie. Her mother wouldn't want her to eat this much, or this early, or this slovenly—in a bed?—and she tries not to think about that because her mother's not here and that's the entire point of college.

The smell of the food slowly brings her back to life, and Frankie finds herself sitting up, wondering what she must look like in her current state. She can feel the tangles in her long, blond hair, feel the makeup from last night's party still caked across her face. Vic had tried her best to help her clean herself up, but at a certain point it was a losing battle, and getting Frankie into boy shorts and an oversized T-shirt and under the covers was as far as they got. Frankie knew, even as it was happening, that she'd take the memory of another woman changing her to her grave. The things people back home would say...

"You don't have to eat if you can't," Vic says, placing a set of plasticwear onto the bed before Frankie, "but at least give it a try. You do have to drink something, though." She holds a cup of orange juice out, hovering it before her, and Frankie recognizes the technique; leave it hanging there in the open air. A small manipulation. To not take it would be rude. Her mother often did something similar, before she simply began ordering Frankie to do things. That came later. After Frankie had shown resistance. Defiance.

"Thank you," Frankie says, taking the cup because she wants to, not because she feels obligated to. Hearing her own voice, feeling the condensation on the plastic cup, makes her suddenly realize how thirsty she is. She pops the top and drinks—slowly, at Vic's insistence. Sipping, not gulping, which is not ladylike.. She wishes her mother's voice in her head would give her just a moment of peace. Frankie pulls the cup away before she chokes, sputtering just a little.

"You good?" Vic asks, her expression is mild; she's asking about the orange juice and not anything else. Not yet anyway.

Frankie and Vic have been roommates since the start of the school year—their junior year, and Frankie's first at Holstenwall College—and they've begun to learn each other's rhythms quite well. Frankie guessed this is what happens when you share a room with someone, when most of the hours in your day are spent around one person. She knows college is supposed to prepare you for the real world, but she wonders if, in some way, it's supposed to prepare you for marriage as well. A trial run, as it were, with the safety of another young woman.

Vic has been at Holstenwall since her first year, and has only cycled through one roommate, which Frankie felt was a good sign. Her previous roomie had moved off campus with a couple friends, and the luck of the lottery had put Vic and Frankie together.

Frankie spent her first two years of college commuting to Parthas Community College, the only school outside her small town in Nevada. Her mother had been upset Frankie didn't choose any Christian colleges, but who was she to say no to the price of community college, or when Holstenwall, one of the most prestigious universities in the country, offered her a free ride for her final two years? She'd told her mother what an excellent opportunity the school was, how great it would look for her (and yes, that was one reason), and her mother begrudgingly agreed.

But another was that New England was a long way away from Nevada.

Frankie grew up near a closed-off, religious

community called Columbia. It was a place that she didn't realize was strange until she started leaving it regularly. Until she started her first job waitressing at a MacReady's fast food chain. Until she started commuting to college.

Until she saw the world outside her world. But she didn't like to talk about that.

It wasn't nice, so she didn't like to talk about it. That was something from home she still hadn't gotten over. Her academic advisor had said, without judgment that the student center offered free, confidential counselling to any student of Holstenwall College, but Frankie had yet to make the trek to that building.

"Whenever you're ready," Vic says, breaking the silence between them. That's all she says, and it's all she's going to say, Frankie knows. They know each other's rhythms. Vic knows Frankie needs time to herself to process what has happened.

But what exactly is it that has happened? Frankie isn't sure. There was a party at the Alpha Chi Epsilon fraternity house, and despite what she's always heard about college parties, about drinking or doing drugs and blacking out, Frankie remembers the entire thing with an unexpected, startling clarity.

But what she remembers cannot possibly be real. Because what she remembers cannot be possible.

She wonders if perhaps someone spiked her drink with some kind of hallucinogen. From a young age, her mother always warned her about Satanists who put LSD into Halloween candy, but Vic was the one who educated Frankie about the much more real threat of everyday men and the kinds of drugs they carried. She had asked Frankie about that on the way home last night. Vic had been half-carrying her, arm around her waist, Frankie's arms draped around her shoulders, simply exhausted from running and sobbing, and Vic told her she was going to ask her something that hurt her. Something that she needed to ask Frankie and would define everything else that was to come.

Did someone do this to you?

No, no, that wasn't what had happened. Even sheltered as Frankie had been all her life, she still heard stories about on-campus assaults. The horrible stories about the raw, red, violent things that went on in dorm rooms or at hazing rituals, about the things that were done to kids by upperclassmen. The things the administration did nothing about because they were crimes committed by athletes; young, white men with their entire lives ahead of them, and so they should be given some grace.

No, what happened last night was something Frankie did, the words of the devil having wormed their way into her ear. It was something that made her hide beneath her covers as soon as she got home. Even though she knew the eyes of Christ above her couldn't really see her through her cheap, cotton comforter, Frankie tried to hide, but she could feel those eyes boring into her. She tried not to think about her mother's disappointed eyes joining in.

Frankie opens her mouth, thinking for a moment that she's going to tell Vic what she's done, that she's going to confess, but she knows that Vic cannot absolve her. Frankie knows that she cannot even wrap her mind around the enormity of it to even say it.

And yet she tries.

"Have you heard of a game called dominion?"

Chapter 2

The Alpha Chi Epsilon house was enormous, its Greek letters looming tall on the side of the building. Frankie stood outside for a long time, hesitant to go in, despite the cold. She finally worked up the courage when another group of students arrived at the house, and she filed inside with them like she was caught up in their wave.

Inside was the college party she expected: blunts being passed around, beer pong, students crowded close together in corners—their limbs intertwined around each other, many of them overtly making out or with hands roaming under layers of clothing. There was an older man in a denim jacket who certainly didn't go there leaning against a wall sipping a beer. Just as it all threatened to overload her, like it all might be too real, too much—a guy with one of those ridiculous beer-can-helmets danced past Frankie, completely unaware of anyone else around him, simply feeling the music. He was so absurd it helped set her at ease.

Frankie was so at ease that she almost didn't think about how her mother would have reacted had she seen the house, the den of sin and debauchery, about the things she would've said had she seen Frankie in such a place. The things she would've done to ensure Frankie never went there again. Despite the lump in her throat at such a thought, there was a part of Frankie that once believed she would have felt the same way had she been confronted with a college party or a shady nightclub or a neon-lit rave. She thought she would have hated it. She thought she would have found the people, the acts, the environment, all of it revolting and offensive. It was an overload to her senses, there was no denying that, but as Frankie moved through the crowded house, as she felt the music worm its way through her body, she felt something unexpected. She felt her heart race, felt herself break out into a smile. She felt...positive. She didn't know exactly how or why, the specificity of the feeling, but she knew this was a good feeling, something she enjoyed and wanted to hang onto, and so she moved deeper into the house.

Frankie took an offered beer from a young woman in a skirt so short it might as well have been a belt. The stranger whooed loudly before continuing through the house, filling each empty hand she saw with a beer can. She handed a couple to the making out couple, to the old man, to beer-helmet-guy. Frankie popped the top and took a sip, and though she didn't love it, she also didn't hate it, and moved into a quieter back room where she'd be able to nurse her drink before wading out into the more rambunctious parts of the party.

"Francesca?"

She flinched at the sound of her full name as soon as she entered the room, but relaxed when she saw it came from Tanner Little, who she recognized as another English major. Tanner was about her height, with mousy brown hair and soft eyes. He, too, held a beer, but was not visibly drunk.

"It's Frankie, actually," she told him. In correcting him, she tried not to think of her mother, but it was impossible because her nickname was chosen in direct defiance of her—a small rebellion, one which Frankie's mother had a disproportionate reaction to. Frankie, Frank, was a man's name, and Francesca should not be using it.

"Frankie," Tanner corrected, "right, sorry. Are you here for what I think you are?" he asked, smiling like they shared a secret.

Frankie swallowed hard.

"Is this where..." she lowered her voice to a whisper, "is this where we play dominion?"

"Hell yeah, it is," Tanner said, and Frankie tried to hide the slight flinch at his use of the word hell. He did not apologize like Vic always did. He didn't know her well enough for that. "How have you heard about that? What have you heard?"

"Just rumors," Frankie said. She heard about it like an urban legend, a piece of Holstenwall lore. It involved the skull of an unknown creature. One with a dozen different, contradicting stories about its acquisition: an archeology student had found it on a trip in the 1920s; some dropout who returned to their old haunt brought it, having won it in a poker game; or, perhaps, the college's first dean in the 1800s had actually hunted the beast while it was alive. Just like any good urban legend, it was all friend of a friend or I know someone who or they go to a different school.

"That sounds about right," Tanner said. "I've heard similar things, rumors nobody has a straight answer to."

Tanner and Frankie chatted for a while before one of the fraternity's brothers, a guy named Kyle who'd drunkenly hit on Frankie a couple times that night, brought the skull out on a soft, velvet pillow, presenting it like an ancient treasure to the eyes of the hushed crowd. Frankie was no biology major, but the bone was unlike anything she'd ever seen. It was definitely not human, perhaps some kind of dog or bear or boar, but she had never seen those thick, curling tusks protruding from the bottom jaw on any animal before. The bone itself was covered in nicks and scratches that were impossible to tell if they'd been gained while the thing—whatever it was—had been alive, or after it had perished.

Kyle held up his hand for silence as he lowered it and its pillow onto the coffee table.

"We usually start off with a little more pomp and circumstance than this," Kyle said, looking over the heads of the crowd to the closed door, and the music thrumming beyond. "I'm sure we'll have all that later, but let's have a little bit of an apertif—" Frankie stifled a smile at his incorrect pronunciation "—before the main event. We can do a little one-one-one swapping, just for fun. But if you wanna play randoms, the rules are simple," he explained. "You put your name in the bowl. Someone else draws from the bowl, and whoever's name they pick, you swap with them. And the swapping itself is the easiest thing in the world. You both just put your hand on the skull and say I grant you dominion."

The gathered crowd chittered with excitement.

"You wanna play?" Tanner asked Frankie.

"Um..." she started, but had no idea what to say. She'd heard the stories about this game before, and assumed it was something related to drinking and drugs. And drinking and drugs she was prepared for. Frankie knew about peer pressure, knew plenty of teenagers in Parthas found ways to get their hands on substances that weren't allowed in the community. But this was something different. This had the vibe of an arcane ritual. This was something her mother would call witchcraft, or perhaps even Satanism directly. And though Frankie knew with her logic-brain she did not believe in such a thing, her emotional brain began to overpower her.

Though, looking at the skull, she realized her fear was not of magic, of whatever strange power this skull was said to possess, but of her mother herself. Of Parthas. Of Columbia. The world she'd left behind. Frankie wasn't afraid of whatever this skull would do to her, but of what they would do if they found out she were in such a place, committing such an act. She thought about the eyes of the crucified Christ.

"Don't worry about it," Tanner waved her off before she could respond to him. His statement was genuine, without the strange duality of communication Frankie had come to expect from many of her peers. "No pressure," he said, "just sit back and watch."

"So," a voice said from behind them, "does that mean you're free?" There was a hand on Tanner's shoulder, and both he and Frankie looked up to find a pretty, young woman in a faded baseball cap, long, brown hair flowing over her shoulders. She wore an authentically-faded leather jacket, a T-shirt of the rock band Darrow Foroi, and those high-waisted mom-jeans that seemed to have come back into fashion.

"Delilah," Tanner said. "Hey, yeah." He introduced Frankie Starling to Delilah Morse, and vice versa, and Delilah sat on the arm of the couch and they watched as the skull made its way around the room, as others played. Frankie watched people recite the words, watched them jitter in place, act strangely once it was all over, euphoric or frightened, touching themselves to figure out who they were. The few movies she'd been allowed to see in childhood that portrayed body swapping (a work of the devil) told her that she should hear the respective voices coming out of the bodies those people now occupied, but of course that wasn't the case.

She didn't know quite what to think as she watched swap after swap, some swapping one at a time, other groups placing their hands upon the skull all together, winding up inside one another at random. At least, that was what they said was happening.

Frankie couldn't figure out if this was all some elaborate prank, if there were drugs or some sort of hallucinogen involved, some scientific explanation she could not wrap her mind around. She was trying to solve it, to explain it, but as the game went on and on, as the rules continued to function exactly how Kyle said they would, she wondered if there was some bizarre version of Occam's razor that had not yet been discovered; the simplest answer was often the correct one, except in this case the simplest answer was magic.

"How long you thinking?" Delilah whispered into Tanner's ear as they watched a whole group switch at random, and then play a guessing game to figure out who was inside who.

"A few minutes?" Tanner asked, admittedly getting nervous the more he watched people switch. What would this be like? How would it feel? He'd already had a couple shots. Would alcohol change the experience?

"Half an hour?" Delilah asked.

"Have you done this before?" Frankie asked,

looking at both of them.

Tanner shook his head, but Delilah nodded.

"What's it feel like?" Frankie asked.

"It's fun as shit," she smiled, watching the group that had just swapped. Someone had clearly swapped genders, and perhaps for their first time, because a blond in tall heels and a tight, black dress was trying to walk across the room, and though Frankie had seen her move with grace earlier, she now wobbled like a newborn deer fresh out of the womb, holding her arms out for balance while her friends cheered her on. Frankie hesitated for a moment, thinking of the way she'd just interpreted that. She just thought the person switched genders. Did she really believe that? Did she think that was what was happening here?

Next to her, Tanner smiled watching the woman because, yes, he found the physical comedy funny, but there was also something else there. Something warmer than humor that he couldn't identify. He wondered if he could balance in shoes like that. He looked over to Delilah and saw she was wearing big, black ass-kicking boots. Maybe next time.

"Half an hour." He offered Delilah his hand, because he didn't really know what else to do to mark a deal like that, and she shook it, smiling in anticipation.

Eventually, Kyle brought the skull around to them, and Frankie retreated into her side of the couch, watching with bated breath as Delilah slid forward, and she and Tanner touched the skull together.

"You ready?" Delilah asked.

Tanner nodded, swallowing hard. Frankie realized she was holding her breath.

Together, Tanner and Delilah said the words I

grant you dominion, and then Tanner felt some invisible hook grab him behind the bellybutton and pull. A heat rushed through him, some kind of flush, a wave of energy he could almost surf, if only he knew how. He felt powerful as that wave crested over him, strong, like for a moment he could channel it, ride it, but then he fell, inexperienced as he was. It felt like he'd taken a drunken stumble and that wave of energy washed over him, moved past him. The moment was gone.

When he pulled his head up again, he was looking at himself.

Literally, across the couch, at himself.

It was strange, but in a different way than he'd expected. The only times you ever really saw your own face were in the mirror, or in pictures, but there he was: sitting in front of himself. And there he was, inside someone else, and he could immediately feel the difference. He felt Delilah's long, dark hair on his shoulders, her baseball cap on his head. He felt the tightness of her shirt across his torso and the denim of her jeans on his freshly-shaved legs. He could feel the differences right down to the molecules; the way her hips swelled and her waist tapered. He could even feel her lips, more plush than his own.

The way he watched Delilah test out his body, he could tell she felt the difference, too. He watched her immediately double over and pull uncomfortably at the crotch of his jeans, trying to unbunch his boxers, and wondered if she could feel the weight of his cock like he felt the weight of her breasts.

"Oh, man, what the hell," she laughed through his mouth, with his voice. She looked around the room. "You guys really can't sit with your legs crossed, huh?"

Everyone burst out laughing; the group, the spectators, watchers from the outskirts of the room.

Beer-helmet-guy, the man in the denim jacket. Even Frankie, albeit a little reluctantly, looking from Tanner to Delilah and back again. She was trying to figure out if this was real, if it had really happened, and if she was being honest she was already beginning to believe.

"You alright?" Delilah asked with Tanner's mouth, looking at him. At herself.

"This is...so weird," he said, looking down at Delilah's hands, wiggling her black-painted nails. He liked them. What did that mean?

"Tanner?"

He looked up as Frankie called his name, and he saw something cross over her face. It wasn't proof, wasn't the full belief that this was real, but she was coming closer to it.

"Is that really you?" Frankie asked.

As Delilah, Tanner nodded. "Yeah," he gasped, unused to the sound of Delilah's voice rumbling in his throat. "Yeah, it's me, holy shit." He didn't apologize, and Frankie found she didn't care.

"You're lucky," Delilah said, leaning back into the couch next to Frankie. She seemed to realize she was sitting next to someone she wasn't as familiar with, and scooched slightly, giving Delilah a bit of a wider berth. "The last time I played this, I swapped with this girl, Jenny Abernathy, who, like, five seconds after she was inside me told me I was about to be on my period."

Frankie watched the skull go around the room, her eyes following it, curious.

Next to her, Delilah used Tanner's hand to motion to her borrowed body, said "Get up and walk around! Take her for a spin!"

Tanner did so, standing tall in Delilah's boots and walking around the room. He didn't figure Delilah weighed much more than him, but even so he could feel the different distribution of weight throughout her body, the way she held onto fat in the hips and thighs and a bit in the upper arms, where Tanner's sat around his middle. He wobbled a little, slouching forward, not used to the feel of breasts and thinking he'd have to compensate for them. He stopped when he caught sight of himself in a mirror in the hall. It was bizarre; moving himself and seeing Delilah move. He brushed her hair out of his face, looking himself up and down.

And then a shape appeared behind him.

"Hey."

"Jesus!" Tanner jumped, surprised by the mirrored sight of Trey Roberts, Delilah's...was he... her boyfriend? Was talking the term people still used for people who were in courtship, but not yet exclusive? Trey was in several classes with Tanner, an Engineering major too, though you wouldn't guess it by his appearance. The first time Tanner ever saw Trey, he thought football linebacker. Which would have been an accurate assessment, if he'd seen Trey in high school. A broken arm hadn't ended his sports prospects, but it had rearranged Trey's mind, told him he'd better have a backup plan. Trey was huge, easily a head taller than Tanner-as-Delilah, and twice as wide, with a mop of messy blond hair.

"Been looking everywhere for you," he said, wrapping his arms around Tanner-as-Delilah from behind, lowering his head so his chin touched their— their?—shoulder.

"Wait," Tanner gasped, pulling away, despite the sudden and unexpected warmth he felt with Trey's arms around him. No one had ever approached him like that before. No one had ever taken him in their arms so directly like that. It made him feel small, but in a good way. Like there was someone there to protect him. Like he was finally allowed to be a tiny, fragile thing. It was that feeling that made Tanner melt into putty when Trey grabbed him by the chin, still standing behind him, and lifted up Delilah's lips for a kiss. Tanner couldn't stop it, didn't want to stop it, felt himself melting as Trey's lips touched his, felt himself leaning back into his embrace, felt himself kissing back.

"Darling," Tanner recognized his own voice, and both he and Trey suddenly turned to see Delilah standing there in Tanner's body. Even though it was him, she still had her own mannerisms, the way she held herself, the wry smile on her face like she liked what she saw. Frankie stood next to her, eyes wide as dinner saucers, her hands clasped gingerly before her, looking like she'd walked in on some indiscretion.

"Oh, shit," Trey looked at the Delilah-coated Tanner. "Oh, shit, I'm sorry...dude?" He looked genuinely embarrassed, and Tanner was surprised and delighted that a homophobic comment, even something as light as no homo, didn't follow.

"That was hot," Delilah said.

Frankie was sure a fight would follow. After all, Delilah's boyfriend had just kissed somebody else. But there was no fight. Not even harsh words. Delilah, in Tanner's body, watched with obvious pleasure in her eyes as her boyfriend put his hands on her borrowed body, his tongue in her mouth. She watched Tanner relent, kiss him right back.

"Are you gonna try?" Delilah asked with Tanner's voice while Tanner and Trey stood next to one another awkwardly.

"I...I don't..." she wanted to say no. Felt like she was supposed to say no—certainly knew her mother and everyone from Parthas would want her to say no. This was the devil's work, something hellish. Witchcraft, at the very least. But what Frankie felt in her belly when she thought about doing what Tanner and Delilah had just done was not a revulsion, but a deep desire. She didn't know if what she wanted to do was swap places with a boy, with Tanner or Trey or even Delilah, but she knew she wanted to explore. She wanted to step closer to this mysterious new desire she'd discovered. She wanted to understand the shape of it.

"There's no pressure," Delilah said, gingerly reaching toward her, but not actually touching her. "If you don't wanna do it, I'll tell the Epsilon dorks to back off and you can stick with beer for the night. Or, if this isn't your thing, we can walk you home."

"No, I..." Frankie looked over her shoulder, back into the room where the game was beginning to get underway. She saw a group of kids all reaching for the skull. "Would you...change with me?"

Delilah smiled, and even though Frankie wasn't very familiar with Delilah or Tanner's mannerisms, she knew the smile was something genuine. Not one of someone who got their way, but of someone who was happy Frankie was trying to expand her horizons, as it were.

The skull was coming around towards them.

"If we do," Frankie said, "will you not...use me to... do anything?"

"Of course not," Delilah said. "Your body, your choice."

"I..." Frankie started, trailed off, and then something came up and out of her chest that forced herself to finish. "I'm still a virgin." Why was that the thing? Why did she suddenly jump straight to sex? Of course, she knew, she just didn't want to admit it. It'd been what she'd been thinking all along. The shame of such a status, but also the shame of losing it.

"Oh, honey," Delilah patted Frankie gently on the back, gently rubbing between her shoulders. "That's alright. That's nothing to be ashamed about." She smiled. "I'm not a virgin, so..." her smile became a little more mischievous, "if you feel like getting frisky tonight, why don't you use me as a loophole?"

Slut. Her mother's voice whipped through her head. Whore. Venom spewed at both Frankie and Delilah.

But the sight of the skull, of that strange face, those bizarre teeth, shook that voice from her mind.

Tanner and Delilah switched back, and when it was Frankie and Delilah's turn to change, she followed the instructions exactly like she was told, and it felt like someone picked her up under her arms and threw her like she was a doll. Chucked her right out of herself and into Delilah, and that sudden shift made her feel drunk. And when she managed to right herself by holding onto the couch against which two swapped people were already making out, Frankie realized it was because of the actual physical differences between herself and Delilah. She could feel her; her hair, feel her boobs—they were bigger than her own.

Sometimes, when Vic wasn't in their dorm or when Frankie was alone in the girls' shower, she would stand naked in front of a mirror and look at herself. She'd look at her tiny A-cups or her nonexistent hips or her flat ass and wish she was different. And now, suddenly, she was. Delilah was thick, which Frankie recently learned was a body-positive way of saying fat. Delilah had darker skin than Frankie and bigger breasts and wider hips, and when Frankie was inside her, she could feel all those physical differences like some fundamental force of nature itself had changed.

"Oh my god," Frankie gasped in a voice other than her own, looking down at this alternate form, trying her best to honestly feel what was inside herself. She didn't feel horror, terror, revulsion, disgust, anything negative. She felt...

Curiosity.

She felt excited.

Frankie felt a strange energy coursing through her. It was electric, a current, not sparks, like people talk about in romantic comedies, but like an actual, physical power, and she felt even more of it when she turned towards the tangle of gathered students who had all begun to shed their clothes with a speed that surprised Frankie.

Frankie recalled how bad behavior was explained to her as a child, how sometimes you found yourself being compelled to do something you know is wrong. For so long, she'd been taught about the Devil, that he was the source of those bad things rattling around in her head. But it was Frankie's job, her mother, the church, the world, had always told her, to remain pure. Free from drugs (which she'd tried at a party in college before). Free from alcohol (which she'd imbibed in before she even left Parthas). Free from the temptations of the flesh—until your husband came along.

She felt that power even more looking into that pink tangle of limbs that the crowd had become. She felt stronger in that moment, emboldened, like she could take on the world.

She felt a hand on her back, pushing her gently towards the crowd.

"Tell me if you wanna tap out," Delilah said, pushing Frankie just a couple steps closer, close enough that she could reach her own hand out and touch the first proffered face. It belonged to a chubby, redheaded woman balanced on an ottoman on her hands and knees. Frankie felt the warmth of her cheek and then gasped in surprise as the woman took Frankie's fingers in her mouth and sucked on them, swirling her tongue around them slowly.

Goddamn, it felt good.

Frankie suddenly withdrew her hand, lifted them both to her mouth, shocked at her own blasphemy. Who could she blame for these acts, these temptations? The other students? The devil whispering in her ear? No, this was of her own free will. This was something Frankie didn't just want, but something she needed. So, then why did she still feel so bad about it? Delilah was her loophole.

"It's okay," the redhead said. "I won't bite." And then, with eyebrows raised, "You want me to bite?"

Frankie held her hand out again.

Gently, the woman took her fingers in her mouth. Gently, she bit down, just enough to make Frankie flinch, but not enough to pull her fingers away. As the woman playfully bit and sucked and swirled her tongue, Frankie wondered if this was even really a woman whose eyes she was looking into. She wondered at the vast possibility of forms before her, but suddenly her mind went blank as she saw a young man stumble out of the crowd, pull his penis out of the hole in the front of his boxers, and seamlessly slide it into the redhead from behind.

The woman gasped and then choked as the man's first thrust pushed her forward, Frankie's fingers sliding down her throat. She gagged and sent a glob of spit into Frankie's palm, her mouth releasing her fingers, and Frankie took a step back and watched in shock as the woman turned to look over her shoulder.

"Who's that back there?" she asked as the man thrust into her.

"Kyle," the man said, though it was most definitely not Kyle's body who'd mounted her.

"Katrina," she said, and Frankie realized she had no idea if this redheaded woman was Katrina, or if this body was borrowed.

Kyle's eyes widened at the name, as if he was surprised this was who he was inside, and he suddenly held onto her tighter, thrusting harder into her. "Oh, shiiiiit," Kyle suddenly gasped, pulling him out from Katrina's insides and shooting ropes of white goo onto her butt.

Frankie took a step back in shock, again lifting her hands to her mouth, but when she did, she realized how much of Katrina's spit was on her fingers, was dripping down her palm, her wrist.

And before she knew what she was doing, she had her hand down her pants, her spit-slicked fingers touching between Delilah's legs.

Good Lord, it was the best sensation she had ever felt in her life. It was not even close. Frankie stuck two fingers inside herself and then longed to know what it would feel like to have someone else do it. She fumbled inexpertly with Delilah's clothes, and when the redhead, who was still on her hands and knees on the ottoman, asked "You want some help with that, honey?" Frankie stepped forward and let herself be undressed.

"Lay down," the redhead said, lowering Frankie down onto the couch, where she pulled off her pants and then her underwear and then lowered herself between Frankie's legs, where her mouth gave Frankie a religious experience. She recognized the feeling of orgasm, had coaxed herself to and over the precipice on nights she was absolutely sure her mother was asleep and she could remain quiet by shoving her face into a pillow. But this was another level, something entirely new. It almost felt like she had to pee, and she thought she did, but it was at the same time she came, fluids shooting out of her and splattering onto the redhead's face.

"Attagirl!" she shouted, pulling away from Frankie's crotch.

"More," Frankie said quietly, so quietly she thought it might've been to herself, and then, louder, "More. Please. Again."

The redhead wiped her mouth, stepping back, and was replaced by a young, blonde man who took over her duties. Frankie was surprised, wanted to retreat, but for some reason, she didn't.

She felt free in that moment. She had never imagined having more than one sexual partner, let alone two at the same time, and as the young man's tongue worked on her, she felt that strange, crimson power from the moment she entered Delilah's body flow through her again.

Sometime in the middle of being satisfied, Frankie opened her eyes and saw another naked man nearby, his penis dangling free, pointed at her like some sort of heat-seeking missile.

Touch it, a voice within herself told her. Touch it. Grab it. Taste it.

And she did. She took the man with one hand and pulled him closer, putting him in her mouth, tasting a penis for the very first time, while someone else grabbed her free hand and slid two of her fingers into a waiting, wet hole.

This was sin?

No, absolutely not. It couldn't be.

Could it?

Could the eyes of Christ see what she was allowing to be done to her, the holes she was filling in this borrowed body? The fear came rushing back at her; the thought that God hads seen what she's done, and knew her sin, and will punish her for it.

When you get to college, you keep those little legs of yours closed.

Frankie looked through the curtain of bodies to where Delilah sat on the edge of the couch, gently rubbing the inside of her thigh. That's okay, she thought, you can do that. But only that. Don't let anyone else touch me. She meant to keep an eye on herself, but Frankie lost herself in the orgy, in the mess of tongues and cocks and cunts, and only a few times did her mind wander and become aware of the vulgarity of her inner monologue, waves of increasing pleasure annihilating the guilt.

She was much more aware of the sudden throbbing in her mouth, of the spurt of warm goo down her throat. Frankie gagged and spit it back up onto the mushroom-head it came from, but after the sudden shock was over, she realized she'd quite liked the sensation, and she reached for another. She was aware of something rubbing against her pussy, something that had replaced the sensation of the tongue, and when she looked up she saw a man holding her ankles up, onto his shoulders, while another one rubbed the first's penis against her. When he slid it in, she felt his warmth, and then Delilah was above her.

"Let them come inside you," her own borrowed face said down to her. There was a pleading in her voice that Frankie had never heard from herself. "I'm on birth control. I want to see it."

"Okay." Frankie did, felt hips bucking against her arrhythmically, and then that spent cock was replaced with another that came almost instantly, pulling halfway out as it emptied so that its owner could look down on his (or her?) handiwork. There was another and another, and soon Frankie could feel semen running between her buttcheeks and down her thighs and on her stomach, and what was even more shocking was Delilah lowered Frankie's own face down towards her, and, after a moment of looking into her eyes, after Frankie's nodded permission, kissed her.

It was soft, sweet, not like the hungry, aching needs of the rest of the night's kisses, the ones on her mouth, on her breasts, her hips, her thighs, between her legs. There wasn't even any tongue. Just Frankie and Delilah's lips brushing against one another, soft and sweet, and there was nothing else in all the night's pleasures that matched the tenderness of that high.

"You believe me?" Frankie asks.

She realizes what she's just said, the story she's just told, and it seems insane hearing it aloud.

"Well, yeah," Vic says, as if it were the most obvious thing in the world.

Frankie's so shocked it takes her a moment to utter, "Why?"

"Frankie," Vic scoffs. "No offence, but have you seen you? You're a straight-A girl, you're never late for anything, I always see you in bed before ten o'clock—with a sleep mask on, might I add. In the olden days we would've called somebody like you a square. There may have even been some, certainly not me, who held you upside-down and dunked your head in a toilet."

Frankie smiles, despite everything. Those words coming from anyone else would've seemed absurd, they would've hurt, and very likely would have been designed to hurt. But coming from Vic, they're affectionate. Vic had once told Frankie she wished she could be more like her, and they both knew she genuinely meant it.

"Besides," Vic continues, her tone shifting darker, "when you called me, it was three in the morning and you were sobbing so hard I could barely understand you, clearly fucked up, and you were on top of the goddamn library—sorry for saying 'goddamn.'"

"It's okay."

"In short, yes, I believe you, because you're not the kind of person to make up something like that. And," Vic says, leaning closer and putting her hand on Frankie's knee, enunciating every word, "you. Did. Nothing. Wrong."

Before Frankie realizes she's doing it, she's leaning across the bed, pulling Vic into a tight hug. Vic's eyes widen in surprise, but she can see the need in her friend's face, and she leans into it, the two of them awkwardly shifting their legs so they can hold each other close, squeezing tight around shoulders, faces buried into necks. Frankie realizes it's her first big instance of physical touch since last night, and it feels good to have her own skin under her again. To have Vic against her, it feels safe.

"I got you, babe," Vic says into Frankie's hair. "Don't worry, I got you."

Chapter 3

"Will you take me to church?" Frankie had asked the next morning.

They'd fallen asleep together, both completely exhausted, on top of Frankie's covers. When Frankie realized what had happened, she struggled to keep from imagining what her mother would say about such a predicament. When she was a child, sleeping in the same bed as her girlfriends was no big deal. But as she got older, her mother policed Frankie's physical touch more and more.

"Of course, sweetheart," Vic had replied, and when it was clear Frankie meant right now, even though it wasn't Sunday morning, they both got dressed, ready to brave the cold of a New England winter.

Frankie's winter gear wasn't very different from her normal outfits; oversized shirts, sleeves drooping down past her fingers, sweatpants that she swam in. They were clothes that did their best to hide her form. Whenever Frankie dressed, she could hear the voice of her mother or her priest back in Parthas, telling her to cover herself—she didn't want to tempt any of the eyes out there in the world.

She can't imagine who she might have tempted last night.

As they walk out of their dorm tower and out onto campus, Vic takes Frankie's arm and snakes it inside the crook of her elbow like she's some sort of old-timey gentleman. The snow still coats the ground, and even this early on a Saturday, the campus is beginning to empty out for the winter break. The lamps lighting up the walkways are lit, and combined with the intermittent snowfall and fog, everything takes on a hazy, dreamlike glow.

Holstenwall remains one of the oldest colleges in America, many of its buildings dating back hundreds of years, erected in styles that make Frankie think of old, fairy tale pictures. A lecture hall laid out in a circular pattern like an old medical examination hall, cobblestone walkways threading through the campus, Tudor-style buildings with snow-topped turrets. The campus has kept with the times, of course; modernizing older buildings and adding new ones, but always maintaining that distinct european vibe. It looks like a place out of time, with strange, added anachronisms like electric walkway lights, blue campus police alert pillars, thermostats and keycard swipes tacked onto old, stone buildings.

Holstenwall's traditional vibe exists not just in its architecture, but in its attitude, as well. This is a big draw, not just for its students, but also their parents. The thought of giving their child an elite education without them ever leaving the continent is a strong incentive. Many of Holstenwall's prospects, especially its liberal arts students, see it as a four-year bohemian escape from the modern world. Which it is, depending on their study of choice. Part of that attitude comes from the school's comparatively relaxed reading weeks—infamously known as hell weeks almost everywhere else in America—which sends Holstenwall's 5000 students to the library to cram for finals. Students are allowed to leave campus for Christmas, if they finish their tests early.

Frankie has finished all of her midterms, and thinks, but only briefly, about returning to Nevada for Christmas. While money is certainly a contributing factor, it's far from the only one. The thought of going home to her mother, to her local church's annual Christmas play with its frightening, uncanny, papier-mâché God-head—it all seems far too much.

Vic didn't plan on heading home either, and she offered Frankie the much more palatable option of buying turkey sandwiches from the local grocery store and streaming a bunch of unconventional Christmas movies on her laptop in bed. She already had Gremlins and Batman Returns in the queue, neither of which Frankie has seen, because her mother had labeled them as Satanic, and not allowed them in the house.

What about Die Hard? Frankie had asked. Not that she's seen that either, but she's heard about it. That's supposed to be the one everyone talks about. It seemed far more violent, but less devilish, and she wasn't sure if that was a trade-off or not. Vic told her it was played out by now.

Holstenwall College has its own church, but because it's not a Christian college, it's technically called "a nondenominational worship center" or something mouthy like that—neither of them can remember the correct terminology. It's equipped with the vestiges of Christianity, Judaism, Islam,

Hinduism, Buddhism, and more. Like most of the rest of the college, the church is old—the oldest building on campus, in fact. When the Town of Holstenwall was founded, before the United States even properly existed, it was meant to be a haven from religious persecution; a place for intellectualism and reason to exist alongside the spiritual.

"You want me to go in with you?" Vic asks.

Frankie nods.

"I...just want to talk to a priest," she says, and she can see Vic's eyes widen slightly. She knows Vic didn't grow up with much religion, so talking to a priest is a somewhat extreme reaction from her point of view. But for Frankie, talking to a priest is just another Saturday morning, a fact of everyday life.

"I won't be long," Frankie says, and together they walk inside.

The doors of the church—Frankie has to stop calling it that, that isn't what it is, even if it is what it was—are never locked, and so they walk right in, taking in the familiar sight of the pews, the altar, the cross hanging above. Most of Holstenwall's religious students belong to some denomination of Christianity, so the largest room is reserved for their worship. There are doors that branch off to the left and right, and Frankie knows if she goes down some of those halls she'll find slightly smaller rooms reserved for the college's Jewish and Islamic believers, and the smaller populations of everyone else.

It's what it looks like on a military base, Vic, the Army brat, had once told her.

"I'll wait here," Vic says, taking a seat in one of the rear pews and pulling out her phone.

Frankie walks up the center aisle, spying the confessional booths to the left. The doors to all of them are open, and she sees no one inside, but before she can even call out, a door at the rear of the pulpit opens, and a priest emerges, engaged in another task, looking at a folder in his hands. He's a tall man with wire-framed glasses and a head full of curly hair.

"Hello," he says, noticing Frankie. "Can I help you?"

Frankie opens her mouth to say something, but for some reason the words come harder now. She's in the presence of what's familiar, of what's supposed to calm her, absolve her, and yet she still feels the same anxiety. She can feel her mother looming behind her, telling her that if she ever did anything bad, God will know. She can feel the eyes of the crucified Christ. All she can do is gesture vaguely to the confessional booth.

"Oh, of course," the priest says with a smile, and waves her inside.

With the doors shut and Frankie closed into the booth, she faces the sudden reality that she's going to have to admit what has happened, what she's done.

When you go to college, you keep those little legs of yours closed.

Her thoughts drift back to the party, the frat house, and the wave of guilt that washes over her is so sudden and intense that the words spill forth unbidden, before she even introduces herself or says how long it's been since her last confession.

"Last night I engaged in Satanic practices," she says quickly, as the memory threatens to overtake her, guessing now that any attempt at subterfuge or massaging the truth is no longer an option. She remembers the words they recited as part of the ritual, I grant you dominion, remembers the skull that the fraternity brothers brought out on a velvet cloth, its tusks curling upward. She remembers touching it, and not just everything that happened after, but every pleasure she felt.

Whore.

Frankie remembers the guilt, and it sits atop her shoulders even now, like a gargoyle, but she also remembers how good the night felt, and she doesn't know what part of her is stronger: the urge to do it again, or the urge to seek repentance.

Frankie's hands rise up reflexively to cover her mouth, but the words are already out and they keep coming, and she can't stop them, even with her hands in front of her lips. She tells the priest about the skull, the bacchanalian ritual, about her becoming someone else, about their repeated, unprotected sex.

Frankie thinks of her mother, tries not to think of the things she'd say, should she ever get wind of this confession. She holds herself, realizes she's shaking, not because of the winter cold, but because of tension.

Because of fear.

But also because of pleasure; growing warm between her legs with the memory of the things she did and the things that were done to her, how in those moments she felt so free, so untethered.

The priest is oddly silent, even after she finishes her long monologue about the night, and Frankie doesn't know what that means. Is he horrified at her sin? Is he simply digesting it? Is there any way he would be able to get word to her mother? It is a lot to hear, after all. Has he ever heard anything like this? He must have, with the Epsilon house so close, the game so popular. There were dozens of students there, and there must've been dozens before. Frankie can't have been the only one to ever visit that house and then come looking to unburden herself here.

"Father?" she asks, desperate, not simply for his approval, for his forgiveness, but for something, anything now that he's been still so long. A movement, a twitch. Something that would let her know he's still alive in there. Frankie can see a vague outline of him through the latticework. Part of her wants to grab the tiny sliding window and pull it aside, to look at him. Has he...fallen asleep against the wall of the booth?

"Father?" Frankie asks again.

He moves, jolts as if he had been asleep, and his sudden movement startles her.

"Are you alright?"

"Oh, yes," he says, but his voice is different, gravelly, like he's trying to hold back a cough.

Frankie swallows the lump in her throat she didn't realize was there.

"It sounds like you had a very fun night," says the priest, and Frankie can see him turning towards her, looking at her through the small window between their booths, "A very eventful night."

He reaches up and grabs the window, slides it open so he can look in on Frankie clearly, but what's on the other side isn't the priest with his curly hair and wire-framed glasses. It's a different man entirely, with long, gray hair; stringy and greasy, like it hasn't been washed in weeks. His eyes are bright, but terrifying, hungry, and drool drips from a yellow-toothed mouth that's wreathed in a scraggly beard.

"I wish I'd been there!" the imposter priest shouts. He lifts himself forward, face-first, as though he means to squeeze himself through the window, but his head is too large, bumping up against the frame, and nevertheless he tries to push himself through. "How many times did you come, little Frankie?" he laughs. "You have to tell me, and then you have to do a Hail Mary for each one." The priest leans back and then reaches his arm through the window. "You have to tell me or I'll tell your mother what you've done!"

Frankie, finally in control of her limbs again, screams and cries and flies out of the booth like a bat out of hell.

Vic is already there to catch Frankie as she spills out of the booth, looking in as Frankie points and screams, half-running, half-crawling away, shouting unarticulated gibberish, unable to form the words to describe her horror.

But the confessional booth is empty. There is no man. No one in the church except for Vic and Frankie and the echoes of Frankie's screams.

Tanner Little is in the middle of a crisis.

He's about to go on his first date with a guy and he has no idea what to wear. He stands before the small mirror hanging on his dorm room wall, lifts what feels like the thirtieth shirt up in front of him, imagining how it would look on his frame, and feeling like it's the wrong choice yet again. He tosses it aside into the pile of clean laundry with a groan that is less exasperated, and begins to cross over into genuine anger.

Tanner has been on plenty of dates with girls. He doesn't keep a body count, like so many of his classmates (personally, he finds comparing body counts to be borderline sociopathic, and, at least, certainly misogynistic behavior), but he's slept with plenty of girls, both in high school and college. He's kissed a couple boys on a couple dates and at a couple parties, but never gone farther than that.

So, then why is he so nervous now?

Tanner has upended his entire dorm room looking for the right outfit. It's nearing Christmas in New England, and so Tanner finds himself faced with the classic date problem of whether he wants to show off his outfit and be cold, or zip up his thick, featureless winter coat and be warm. At least until they make it inside the restaurant.

Though the real issue at hand is not just the look of all of his potential outfits, but the feel. Every single shirt or pair of pants Tanner tries on scratches at his skin, like a thousand tiny fingers with untrimmed nails poking at him from every conceivable angle, determined to make him as uncomfortable as possible. Tanner stands in the middle of his dorm room in his boxers, the only piece of clothing that doesn't make him feel terrible. It's strange, the clothes he tries on don't just feel ill-fitting physically, they feel wrong emotionally, if that's possible. It's something Tanner's felt before, but never as strong as this. Before, it's only ever been the sudden spike of a sensation—wrong—when he throws a shirt over his head in the morning. He's never stayed with that feeling long enough to dissect it, simply tossed that shirt aside and picked a new one that felt right, sometimes not getting it until after a couple tries. He knows some friends who've had that same experience from time to time, a weird sensory day.

But not all of his friends have had the experience Tanner has had lately. The experience that seems to have ramped up this occasional uncomfortable feeling inside his head to a near-constant buzz.

Not all of his friends have played dominion.

Tanner's mind has felt like this—completely scrambled—ever since that night at Alpha Chi Epsilon. He'd heard about the game before, even witnessed it in action a couple times, but never had he himself played it until recently. It took watching the event a few times to convince him of the game's supernatural implications.

Kids in college, or at least the ones Tanner knows, don't really go on dinner dates. They usually go drinking or partying. They skip most of the date part of the date, and just get right to the hookup. Had Tanner been going on dates with girls, he may have also done so. But this is a new experience for him, and he wants to enjoy it, to savor it.

Tanner goes out with some guys. One night he ends with a hot, heavy makeout in front of his dorm hall with a guy named Christian, but goes no further, not yet, because Tanner says he is still figuring some things out. Christian is cool with this.

Tanner thinks about that as he lays in his bed that night, alone. His roommate, Brody, went home for the holidays, like so much of the rest of the campus, and Tanner lets his mind drift, fingers inching closer to the plastic waistband of his boxers at the memory of Christian's lips on his, but there's something strange. His fantasies head in a different direction than he expects. He doesn't think about his hand on Christian's cock, or even Christian's mouth on his. Tanner thinks about lying on his back and spreading his legs, about Christian's hips between his thighs, the mechanics of the position and the twisting of his own hips be damned.

He withdraws his hand, shame flushing through him.

This isn't how Tanner thinks he's supposed to feel. Or maybe how he expected he'd feel. It's not them, the boys he's seeing. It's him. There's something about Tanner that feels off, something wriggling inside him that he hasn't felt before. It's true that in his relationships he tends to be more dominant with women, more submissive with men, but something about this is different even than that. He feels so much more aware of his body than he ever has, of every single motion and movement, of how he's being perceived outside of himself. He's aware of how his clothes fit on him, of how they feel against his skin, and it seems like every moment of every day, he's adjusting his soft dick in his pants, constantly uncomfortable no matter its position.

Sometimes, when he's alone, he swears he feels the ghosts of Delilah's breasts hanging off his chest. He swears he can feel their weight in the moments before he drifts off to sleep.

But when he dreams, it's not about the skull, or about Delilah or some other version of himself.

It's about that old man, the one who was hanging around the edges of the party.

The dream is always the same; the old man is at one end of a long hotel hallway, running towards him in a stuttering gait, seemingly distracted by the things he sees in the rooms he runs by. Tanner can't see, but from those rooms he hears screams and moans, and he can't tell if they're from pleasure or pain or some combination of both. The old man will slow, his step hitching, and then seemingly remember he's intent on pursuing Tanner, and pick up speed again.

Tanner always wakes before the old man reaches him, always in a sweat, but instead of his torso being entirely coated, like he normally is after an exertion, his sweat forms a new and distinct pattern; almost exclusively pooling on his sternum. As if between breasts.

Is everything he's feeling something to do with the skull and dominion? Some kind of withdrawal symptoms? Or like how LSD is supposed to stay in your system for months or years afterwards? Tanner isn't sure. There isn't exactly any sort of precedent for the idea of touching a magic skull and swapping bodies. Maybe Kyle or Zack would know.

He's crossing the campus, lost in an ocean of thought, when he very nearly bumps into someone.

"Shit, sorry," he says, embarrassed because there are so few people, so much room, and it's so easy to hear everyone coming through the crunch of snow. When he looks up, he sees it's Delilah, followed closely by Trey. A strange, unfamiliar feeling wells up within Tanner then. At first he thinks it's something like finally seeing your crush after a long time apart. The swell is strong and positive, and Tanner feels butterflies in his stomach. But when he thinks about him and Delilah together, there's something off about it, like trying to jam two pieces from different puzzles together. There is still something there, but he doesn't have the words to define it.

"Not even looking at your phone," Delilah says playfully. "Space case."

"Hey," Trey says, "party guy."

"Hey," Tanner says nervously. "Hey, D."

"D?" she says, and he can see a smile blooming on her face, "Didn't know we were that close." The words sound like a joke, but their tone tells him she likes it. Her cheeks are flushed, and Tanner doesn't know if it's because of the cold or something else.

"Well, I've been inside you," Tanner says, suddenly aware of the inappropriateness of the knee-jerk joke in front of Trey, but he laughs even harder than Delilah.

"I don't know how y'all do that," Trey says, looking between the two of them. "Freaks me out."

"The other night wasn't the first time you played, right?" Tanner asks, and he can see they both sense the seriousness that's surrounding him.

Delilah shakes her head.

"Only a couple times," she says.

"You haven't?" Tanner asks Trey.

"Nah," Trey shakes his head, holding up his hands as if he can even keep the notion of it away from him. "Nah, but y'all do you." He looks at them both with that same kind of interest with which Delilah looked at Tanner.

Is he imagining this?

Back to the point.

Tanner looks back to Delilah.

"After you played, have you ever...felt anything weird?"

"Weird how?" It looks like she's trying to suss out what Tanner really means, like she's trying to decode some riddle he's given her, but try as she might to hide it, he sees the spark of recognition in her eyes, the familiarity. The thought that someone else has possibly experienced what she'had, and the reluctance to not be the first one to talk about it.

"Afterwards," Tanner says. "I've felt..." For some reason he suddenly thinks it sounds stupid, and he's unable to say it.

"Not like yourself," Delilah says. It's out in the open, at least a little more now, and Tanner feels some of that weight lift from his shoulders. He sees it come off Delilah too.

"Yeah," Tanner says. They're on the same wavelength now, or at least getting closer. "I've...I think I've felt like you," he says, laying it all out there, no matter how it sounds, because once there's even a small hole in the dam, the rest of it has to come forward. "I've felt like being you again."

Delilah looks down at her shoes, and Tanner doesn't think she's going to say anything, that it's all going to be over, that he's fucked up and guessed wrong, but Trey nudges her shoulder. She looks up at him, tears welling in her eyes.

"Go on," Trey urges, and in those two soft

words Tanner can tell this has been between the two of them for as long as he's been feeling it, maybe longer.

Delilah looks at Tanner.

"I've felt like you too."

And with that, Tanner can feel a bridge being slowly built across the chasm between them.

Frankie doesn't often drink, and she certainly doesn't often drink at a time that ends in A.M., but when they make it back to their room, Vic pours her a shot from a bottle of whiskey that she's not supposed to have in a dorm and tells her just one, that it'll calm her nerves a bit. Frankie doesn't decline it, but neither does she take the shot all at once, instead taking small, steady sips, the plastic cup shaking in her hand. What's been happening lately, how have the stars aligned—the stars have nothing to do with it, don't you talk that witch-talk, says her mother's voice—that they keep finding themselves in this position again; Frankie sitting on her bed, traumatized by something, and Vic waiting for her to open up about it.

Vic is quiet while Frankie collects herself, slowly feeling the shaking in her limbs quiet.

Slowly, deliberately, she tells Vic what happened.

Vic takes the whole story in, eyes never leaving Frankie's, not until she's finished her story, and when she is and she's crying, Vic wraps her arms around her, and they fall asleep together.

Frankie and Vic don't move much over the next couple days, spend most of their time in one or the others' beds, watching their off-kilter Christmas movies. Batman Returns (warped, compliment), Gremlins (bizarre, lovely, but with one deeply unsettling monologue), and even Die Hard (fell asleep).

Frankie ignores the repeated buzzing of her phone, especially because most of the messages are either from her mother, or Kyle Millner of Alpha Chi Epsilon, who has managed to find her on Instagram and hit her with some very sub-standard pickup attempts and vague allusions to inviting her to playing more rounds of dominion.

She lets her phone battery die.

Vic doesn't ask her about the man in the confessional again and Frankie doesn't bring him up, because she's not so sure he even was a man. That he was even real. Even though she knows this is no solution, she tries to lose herself in their deluge of bizarre holiday movies, and pretend he doesn't exist, burying that memory alongside all the others she can't bring herself to confront.

Chapter 4

Dominion hasn't ever been a real problem before, but Kyle Millner hears that some brothers are saying it might be now, after their last session. There are rumors someone's talking after the party the other night, and even though Alpha Chi Epsilon has escaped some pretty serious punishments in the past, they're on thin ice now. You can only have so many close calls. And even fewer close calls around a frat. Not fair that frats are singled out like they are, but that's the world they live in now.

Epsilon should probably stay away from the huge ragers for a little while, stick with their private games like Go Fuck Yourself. Not one of Kyle's favorites, but one he's played a couple times. Everybody would use the skull to switch, randomly, and then you had to have sex with whoever was in your body. It was more about the experience, not always about winning, but sometimes they made a game from it. If you couldn't bring yourself to do it, you were out. Whoever could last the longest won.

Sometimes they simply raced, swapped and then tried to see who could come first in a new body. Shit like that. Hell, the initiation rite to even get into Alpha Chi had the pledges, one by one, swap with a brother's girlfriend, and she'd use their borrowed bodies to blow her boyfriend. Just for fun one night, Kyle had swapped with Zack's girlfriend Heather, and while he'd been Heather he'd blown Zack while Heather used Kyle's body to jerk off onto her own borrowed ass. That was the first time Kyle had ever sucked anyone's dick, the first time anyone had ever cum on him. He didn't hate it, but he hasn't done it again in his own body, only when playing dominion. He wasn't gay, nothing like that, but he was in college, after all. Time for a little experimentation.

But there are always some people out there who have a problem with just having a little fun.

If you believe the rumors (which Kyle doesn't), people who've played dominion have begun seeing things. Having post-game hallucinations like people have LSD flashbacks. Kyle himself played dominion plenty of times before. Hell, he'd played it at the very party that seemed to be the center of controversy and he hasn't been seeing anything. Well, not counting the things he'd seen when he was on shrooms.

There was that old guy, one of the visions people seem to be whispering about, but Kyle doesn't think he was a hallucination.

The night of the game, Kyle had done shrooms before it all started, curious to see if he could take their effect with him while he jumped, or if it would remain in his body when he left it behind. As far as he knew, no one had ever really tried anything like that before. No one knew if it would work, mostly because everyone who played dominion was already drunk or high by the time the game started. With the shrooms in his system, he'd seen the standard wriggling walls and corporeal melding of individuals he usually got.

But there was also the guy. Creepy-looking old guy who hung out around the edges of the game. Long, gray hair like a hippie, unshaven, flannel shirt and a vest. Clearly not a student, but neither was he getting involved with the festivities, never inching closer to any of the writhing bodies. Not trying to play, just looking like he wanted to get a good look at it all. The guy had watched the skull, his eyes lingering on people after they jumped. A voyeur, Kyle guessed. Everyone had their kink, and he wasn't about to shame.

That kind of thing happened sometimes, people wandering into frat parties off the street. Especially with guys like that, old men past their prime who wanted to relive their glory days. And there's always some desperate chick with daddy issues or another who swooned whenever the guy flashes a smile and keys to a Porsche. The dude was probably just there to fuck some sorority chick who would put in far more effort in the sack than a woman his own age would and Kyle had no beef with that.

But who he does have beef with, even if it's incidental, are the people who are talking. He was there that night, for that party, and knows it didn't get any more out of hand than these things normally do. But you never can be too safe, especially these days, when accusations are getting thrown around every other day, and it's now his job to go and check on Frankie Starling, the girl who blew out of the party as the skull's effects wore off, because she isn't answering any of his DMs.

Kyle remembers her from the night of the party. Remembers her vividly. From time to time,

Alpha Chi Epsilon got those cute, quiet girls; the ones who heard the legendary stories about the parties or the rumors about the skull, and wanted to come see if the stories were true. Most of those girls ended up declining the skull but accepting beers, which was totally fine. They ended up partying just the same.

But Frankie had taken the skull.

Not just taken the skull, but taken it all the way. She'd swapped with Delilah Morse, a girl who was in their Algebra class, and even though Kyle had seen Delilah Morse naked before, had even hooked up with her multiple times without the aid of the dominion skull, there was something different about that night that he didn't understand until quite recently. If he put the two girls in a lineup, if it came down to purely looks, Kyle would pick Delilah over Frankie ten out of ten times. Delilah was thick. Her tits almost spilled over the edge of her bra. Huge ass. And she didn't have those little dimples on her thighs and ass most other big girls did. Frankie on the other hand was skinny and flat-chested. Not that there was anything wrong with that, of course, Kyle was body-positive (you had to say you were these days), but that just wasn't his type. It was just Delilah's personality that grated Kyle. A personality as big as her body. He didn't love that when they were fucking, she was the kind of girl who told him what to do instead of asking him for something.

But the way Frankie drove Delilah's body when they swapped was the best of both worlds. Kyle liked the way she held herself shyly, one hand held down over Delilah's shaved pussy, the other trying to cover her tits as she slowly stepped forward. He liked the way she deferred to others in the room, letting them lead, adjust her, the way she opened herself up to their commands.

Kyle was not even remotely self-aware enough to understand the fetid swamp his brain had long ago drowned in, pushed deep down into the muck by YouTube algorithms that told him how alpha he could be, by blockbuster movies that made women plot devices at best and sex objects at worst. Drowned by men like his father and the notion of trying to get an ever-increasing body count, and even by his own friends who were generally good dudes but said nothing in the face of even the most casual misogyny.

Kyle doesn't take any of his brothers when he goes to look for Frankie Starling, doesn't want to come off as aggressive or pushy, merely concerned. Yeah, that's the right way to go. Ask her if she's feeling alright.

Maybe, Kyle thinks as he pops his earbuds in and turns on Spotify, he'll ask her if she wants to go again, just to prove how safe and fun it is. There've been plenty of times where someone was put off by dominion, who freaked out only to return a few nights later, meekly asking for another go with the skull.

Maybe Kyle will ask if, just to dip her toe in, Frankie wants to be him and he could be her, and they could have a little fun together. She might like that.

Kyle crosses the campus with a privileged, carefree strut, earbuds in, music blaring, obfuscating any outside stimuli, eyes cast down at his phone as he aimlessly scrolls social feeds.

He doesn't intentionally move through patches of light, doesn't hold his keys between his fingers Wolverine-style, doesn't cross open lots when he sees groups of boys in the distance, because he doesn't even bother looking for them.

He moves as if the world revolves around him,

not as if it is a monster waiting for him with open jaws, and he has no idea of the ignorant attitude with which he lives his life.

Delilah's reasons for wanting to revisit dominion are different from Tanner's.

Whereas Tanner unlocked something about his gender the first night he played dominion, Delilah has long ago realized something else. She thinks about what it felt like to see Trey hovering over her borrowed body, the look of her and him, remembered what it felt like to see Frankie walk her into that morass of bodies, and felt a strange charge run through her, something separate from the very obvious and familiar arousal she felt. She liked the thought of watching Frankie—herself—have sex with all those people, and wanted to see it happen with Trey next, almost like if she could see it, it would be like test-driving a potential change in their relationship. That forbidden desire pumped a strange and unfamiliar power through her veins. It made her feel afraid, but it also made her feel strong, limitless, like she could harness it if she just knew a little more about what it was.

Delilah hasn't talked with Trey about it since that night, other than the occasional, whoops, remember that, kinda funny (she knows he isn't a fan of dominion, but he doesn't begrudge her her vices. He'll watch, and seems to like watching, but doesn't partake himself). No, she wants to go into that conversation, whatever it may entail, knowing how she feels about it first, knowing not just what this fantasy is she's thought up, but where that sense of power came from too, before she brings it to him.

But she's had visions as well.

Since she's played dominion, she's seen that

strange man Tanner told her about at more places than just the party at Epsilon. All around Holstenwall campus she sees him. and in ways she thinks can't be hallucinations. Or, at least, not any hallucination she's ever heard about. Her first few sightings of him at the house were of an unsettling, leering man in the crowd, visible, it seemed, only to her. But sometimes around campus, she's seen him from afar, with his back to her. Catching him going around a corner or disappearing behind a hedge. She's never heard of anyone having any hallucinations like that. Not when they're so far removed.

And while Trey believes her about what she's been seeing, she knows it's not as real for him. Not as dangerous. Delilah has never been a serious drug user. Sure, she'd smoked some pot in high school and occasionally college, but the crowd that sold it to her told as many urban legends and falsities about drugs as did the D.A.R.E teachers and the Just say no parents. She has no idea if what she's seen is some sort of drug-induced hallucination that's been laying dormant in her body or what.

She doesn't want to think about the possibility that perhaps it's a genuine hallucination, drugs aside. Delilah has a distant aunt who her family once shipped to a mental hospital in the Pacific Northwest, somewhere they could put her and never talk about her again. There's always been a small part of Delilah that's feared that unknown inheritance.

Of course, there is always the possibility that whatever's happening to them is the result of some kind of germ or bacteria they got from touching an old, gross bone of unknown origin that's spent the last few years hanging around a dingy, disgusting frat house.

So, in order to find answers, the three of them—Delilah, Trey, and Tanner—trudge through the abandoned campus, through the snow, towards the Epsilon house.

Frankie and Vic yet again find themselves crossing a nearly-abandoned campus on their return from the dining hall. Despite the holiday and the absence of most of the students, the campus facilities are all still open, albeit with minimal staff.

While there's something nice about a full campus, about passing students who are here for the same reasons Frankie is, she also likes the quiet, to be alone with her thoughts. Vic isn't the kind of person who needs to fill in empty space, so they walk together without speaking. The only sound is the snow crunching under their boots and the puff of their breath as they trudge, the winter world amplifying even those whispers.

An outing out into the world, even as dreamlike a world as Holstenwall's dark, snow-covered, half-abandoned campus, brings some life back into Frankie. It's like an inverse of the desert walks she would take outside her home in Parthas, where she would see shrubs dotting the dusty landscape, the occasional lizard or armadillo there replaced here with cawing crows or chittering squirrels picking through snow. The campus has that strange, heavy kind of silence that only comes with snow, and Frankie is relieved the voice of her mother isn't filling up that silence, like it often would on her desert walks.

No, her thoughts are busy with someone else's voice.

The voice of that man.

Frankie has, on many occasions, dealt with behavior that she would call harassment, but that her mother, and so many others in Parthas, referred to simply as the way men behave.

Why can't it be both, she wondered then and now. She'd had men catcall her on the street, had boys in her high school stand around her in ways she would call cornering but they would call friendly. Even over dinner with Vic she had to ignore the buzzing of her phone; multiple DMs from Alpha Chi brothers who'd found her various social media accounts, telling her about upcoming parties, chatting about the previous one, sending unsolicited dick pics.

They are taught these things from such a young age.

But Frankie has never experienced anything like that man in the confessional booth before. Which is what makes her think, maybe, it wasn't actually real. After all, where did he go? Why didn't Vic see him? He was a spitting image of the man Frankie saw lingering around the edges of the Alpha Chi Epsilon party, so maybe her hallucination in the confessional booth—if indeed that's what it was— was something like a dream; her brain taking old images and repurposing them.

But deep down, some part of Frankie knew that wasn't the answer.

There are barely any blind spots on Holstenwall's wide open campus, so Frankie and Vic can see one of the few students they pass on their journey suddenly turn and redirect himself toward them. Frankie tenses, feels herself start to close ranks, but Vic is the opposite, puffing herself out, stepping in front of Frankie.

This, too, would constitute harassment.

"Hey!" the kid says, approaching them, and

Frankie recognizes him instantly. Kyle. Kyle Millner. With Alpha Chi Epsilon. Like so many guys, he looks different from his picture on the internet, but she remembers his face from the party. "Hey, Frankie."

"Kyle," she says unenthusiastically, already regretting acknowledging him at all, giving him the opening.

"Good to see you again," he says, but it's obvious this is not a simple greeting, not running into them by chance. "I wanted to talk to you," he says to Frankie. "About the other night."

Of course he's come with a purpose.

Now Vic steps more fully in between Frankie and Kyle, and Frankie feels a swell of gratitude in her heart for her best friend.

Best friend? Is that what Vic is to her? And in so short a time? She must be. After the last couple days, after everything Vic has done for her, it's the only answer there is.

"Please tell me," Vic says, "that you're not about to say what I think you're about to say."

"Uh..." Kyle looks completely dumbfounded, unprepared on every single level for Vic, for a woman to stand up to him. "What do you think I'm about to say?"

Vic responds with something, and they keep talking, their voices escalating, but Frankie is distracted, tunes them out as she sees something over Kyle's shoulder, three more people approaching, one a head taller than the other two.

For a moment she flinches, fearing more Alpha Chi brothers, and then,

"Tanner?" She wonders, but it is him, Tanner Little, Delilah Morse, and her boyfriend (?) Trey Roberts.

Kyle turns around and looks at the newcomers.

"Oh, hey, guys, listen, there's no problem here."

"Didn't say there was," Delilah says, but the way she looks at Kyle says there most certainly is now. She looks to Vic and Frankie, and in her eyes there is the secret, coded language of women, that invisible tongue every woman or femme-adjacent person must learn in order to navigate the world, to communicate with one another in ways men cannot know about.

"We've been looking for you," Tanner says to Kyle, who visibly shifts in relief. Tanner glances over at Frankie, offering her a curt hello, an awkward one after what they saw each other do the other night, but then he gets a proper read of the situation, and tenses. "Kyle," Tanner says slowly, amicably, trying to diffuse whatever it is that's going on. "Can we talk to you? It's important. It's about..." he hesitates, but then says it aloud anyway, "dominion."

"I think that's what this is about too," Vic says, motioning to her and Frankie. "Isn't that right, Kyle?"

"Hey, look, man," Kyle says, a little louder, "I'm not trying to start anything." But some passersby look, slow down, but don't stop. One kid breaks away and begins heading in their direction, and when he gets closer, they all recognize Zack Fort from Epsilon house.

"Well, well, well, what's going on here, familiar faces?" Zack is fashion catalogue handsome, with blue eyes and a clean-shaven face. At Zack's presence, Kyle puffs up, given an emotional boost by the presence of his frat brother. "We thinking about playing another game?" Zack rubs his hands together eagerly.

He looks around at the group, and if Frankie had to categorize his look, it would be hungry. When he looks at Frankie, she can practically see the memory of what he witnessed her do flash through his eyes. She shrinks in on herself, trying not to hear the sound of her mother scolding her, trying not to feel the eyes of the crucified Christ.

"Back off, Zack," Vic says, stepping up to him. "Did you put him up to this?" She points a finger-gun at Kyle that's so accusatory it looks like it might actually go off.

"Up to..."

Delilah and Trey look at one another, an expression crossing between them that clearly says we're missing something.

"Look," Kyle says, "I didn't do anything, all I said was I wanted to talk and that's true." He looks at Frankie, "I DM'd you."

"You sure did," Vic says, "And didn't take the hint when she left you on read."

Voices raise and tensions flare, and Frankie takes a step back as Vic and the frat boys get closer, tighter, more wound up.

The only thing that breaks the tension is when Zack, seemingly growing disinterested with the entire thing, glances out of their circle and says "Who the fuck is this now?"

Everyone turns to follow his gaze. At first, it seems like he's looking at nothing more than another snow-coated corner of campus. But after a moment a shape congeals, stepping forth from the darkness at the base of a hedge and into the light of a sidewalk lamp.

It's a man, older, but not old, with long, gray hair pulled into a top-knot and a few days' worth of stubble. He's dressed in black boots, tight, leather pants in the winter for some reason, and a vest over a flannel shirt, a getup that makes him look like an aging rocker. His vest is dotted with patches and pins, his fingers wrapped in rings, but the students are too far away to see their details. What they can see, the horrid sight their eyes seem drawn right to, as if by gravity, is the man's hard penis outlined against his pants. As the man approaches them, he smiles, wide and terrible, a smile that's the challenge of the animal kingdom, not the greeting of the human world.

It's him. The man from the frat party. The man from the confessional booth. The man from Tanner and Delilah's dreams. The face that's been following them all. None of them would ever forget those lingering, lecherous eyes.

"Hey, that's the guy!" Kyle says.

Zack puffs out his chest, wading through the center of the group to face the man.

"Yo!" he shouts, steadily approaching. More like marching. "What's your problem, my dude?"

"No problem," the man says, despite continuing to smile like he wants this confrontation very much. "No problem at all."

"What's your beef?" Zack asks, stepping right up to the man, who is seemingly unaffected by the cold, not shivering. To Frankie, it doesn't look like he's even breathing. She can't see any steam coming out of his mouth when he talks. "Who are you?"

"My name is Joseph Idlu."

"Well, Joseph Idlu," Zack says, "we're tryina have a private conversation here. What are you doing peeping around a college campus? I know you don't go here."

"Do you?" the man, Idlu, asks, smile suddenly wiped from his face, all friendliness gone from his voice. "Are you sure of that?" Another moment of silence. "I mean, can you prove it?"

Zack says nothing for a moment, taken aback by the challenge. Behind him, Kyle looks aghast, wondering if his leader is really going to stand for this.

"Vic," Frankie whispers, tugging on Vic's sleeve. "We need to go. Right now." She looks at Tanner, Delilah, and Trey. "Come on."

Vic gives her a look like she knows this is going to go downhill quickly, like this situation is going to escalate into something they don't want to be around for. Frankie gestures with her chin over Vic's shoulder, noting the nearby campus security call tower, a ten-foot blue pillar with a single, big button that places a direct call to campus security. Despite the empty campus, there's always someone stationed. The whole group slowly sidles towards it.

When that man Idlu speaks again, it's in a whisper, but his voice somehow carries, somehow works its way into the ears of every single person there like he's standing right behind them, even though his words are only meant for Zack; "Can you prove it...like I can prove you have my skull?"

Zack tries not to show it, but he flinches.

"What are you talking about?"

"I'm talking about the skull you have in your bedroom closet. The one you stole from the cab of that big rig on 66 after you failed to win it in that poker game. The one that now you use to play that little game with your friends."

"How—how the fuck do you know that?" Zack growls.

Idlu doesn't answer. He only says "Use it again," smiling again, stepping closer to Zack. "Wasn't it fun? You should do it again."

"Listen, old man," Zack says louder than he needs to, clearly meaning for everyone to hear, "I have no idea what you're talking about! I've never stolen anything in my life."

Frankie reaches out and grabs Vic's sleeve,

desperate to hang on to something as their group turns their walk toward the blue call tower into a more of a hustle. They can all tell it's going wrong, that something very bad is about to happen.

"I've had enough of you, old man," Zack says.

Vic skids to a stop next to the tower, slipping on the snow. Frankie right behind her, looking over her shoulder.

"Fuck this," Tanner says, right behind them. He's holding hands with Delilah, who has her other hand firmly in Trey's, their whole group desperate to cling to one another as if a storm is about to hit. "Let's just leave."

Vic jams the blue button. Over and over again. A swirling, blue light on the tower bursts to life, but there's no siren.

Zack pushes Idlu. Once. Hard. Not hard enough to knock him over, but hard enough to make him stagger.

There is a long silence.

"Well." Idlu says, looking down at his chest as if he can see the residual handprints of where Zack touched him. "That's okay. You can't get your dick wet every night. Sometimes you just have to settle for hand stuff." He lifts his hand and swipes it open-palmed in front of Zack's face, like he's slapping him, but no one hears the loud pap of palm-on-cheek.

Instead, there's a wet, gurgling noise. The sound of a splatter.

The static-filtered voice from the blue tower says "Campus security—" but it's cut out by the hideous, high-pitched scream coming from Kyle. But not Zack though. No, Zack would never make another noise again.

Everyone huddled over by the blue tower watches as Zack slowly turns with the momentum of Idlu's strike, revealing a red, open wound on his throat. Or, rather, where his throat used to be. The entire thing is torn away, leaving nothing but a bloody, red canyon the size of a fist.

The splatter sound, it was the blood hitting the snow. It steams at Zack's feet, sizzling as it's exposed to the cold air. Zack lifts his hands up to his throat, but there's no way he can ever hope of staunching the wound. He staggers for a moment, lifting his hands away, holding them out for balance, but that only lets him bleed more, and he falls, drops to one knee and then faceplants in the snow.

Behind him, Idlu holds up a hand as if inspecting it. But it's not a hand anymore. They can't see past the blood and viscera coating it, but they can see that it has changed, grown larger, the size of a catcher's mitt. The fingers and thumbs now, instead of ending in nails, each terminate in an enormous, curved talon. But there aren't enough of them. And the texture is different, not skin, but they can't tell exactly what past all the blood and gore. It looks like someone has chopped off the man's hand and Frankensteined on an entirely different limb, the four-clawed talon of an enormous bird of prey.

He swipes at Kyle with that talon and it catches him across the chest, sending him spinning into a nearby bush, screaming and bleeding.

Somewhere, someone is screaming into the speaker on the blue tower, calling for help, but it's impossible to tell who, multiple voices overlapping, pleading for help, saying someone's dead and someone else is probably dead too and there's a monster please send help Jesus God.

There's something else then. Something in the darkness beyond the lit campus walkways that rears up behind Idlu. An enormous, dark shape, darker than the darkness, pulling in all light. It's behind him, but it's somehow also part of him, not a separate entity, but like they are getting the smallest glimpse at the real Joseph Idlu, whoever this man really is, reaching toward them from somewhere else, somewhere far and forbidden and awful.

The shape rears up behind him and Frankie recognizes its head.

So does Tanner.

So does Delilah.

It's the skull. The same exact shape each of them laid their hands on in order to play dominion. They'd recognize it anywhere; that piglike snout, those monstrous tusks sprouting from the face. Massive, shadowy shoulders bookend the head as it leers down on the group, every single one of them frozen to the spot in complete and total terror.

Joseph Idlu laughs as taloned hands reach out, grabbing Zack Fort's body, knife-like nails digging into it, dragging it into the darkness, and what follows is a terrible, defiling, wet, slurping sound.

Frankie is dimly aware of someone lifting her off her feet, carrying her away, but she can't take her eyes off of Idlu, off that terrible, monstrous shape in the dark—of the dark.

Wiping the college boys from his lips, the thing that calls itself Josef Idlu looks out at the options before him like a man at an all-you-can-eat buffet, the choices he's narrowed down, in the form of a gaggle of college students fleeing the scene of his true identity. There are so many delicious options and he doesn't know which to savour first.

There's Delilah; the one he discovered first among this group, the leather-jacketed girl he imagines he could ride for years until he got tired of her. He's already wrung some pleasure out of her, taunting her with that desire she's unable to admit to yearning for. He's appeared to her in her dreams as a threshing maw of limbs, herself at the center, grunting and screaming with forbidden pleasure as formless shapes penetrate her every drooling hole. She's woken up with her underwear soaked, liquid streaming down her thighs, and she's felt a sense of shame whose origin she cannot determine, and felt even more shame when she couldn't resist laying back down into that wet spot, putting her hand between her legs, trying to relive that dream as if it were a memory.

Another option is Tanner, the child who knows, deep down, what they are, even if they don't understand it yet, or are unwilling to admit it. Idlu can feel, coursing through Tanner, a similar fluid energy that runs through many members of the Lupanar. There are some members of that ancient order, unbound by the limits of the flesh, who've stitched themselves into hermaphoditic angels, or who've shed their old skin entirely, casting aside useless sex organs for new, preferred ones (Idlu has no quarrel with any of them because of the fluidity or identity, only because of their pompousness, their arrogance). But despite the beauty, the truth, the joy in such a revelation that Tanner was about to crest, there was very often trauma to go on the side.

And trauma tastes so good. Nearly as good as chymos, the flowering, red, carnal energy that is his primary sustenance. The humans have called it many things throughout history; vitalism, qi, humors, and it is not a delicacy exclusive to the Lupanar. Anyone can partake in it. He's seen humans harness it dozens of times. The Marquis de Sade, Vātsyāyana, Pope Alexander VI. For good and ill. Or, perhaps more accurately, selfishness and selflessness.

Yes, he thinks, that's more accurate.

Idlu has long thought of mastering chymos as the human equivalent of adding gravy onto meat, toppings onto ice cream, spices to a dish. That boy he ate in the quad didn't have much trauma, and what little he did have was buried deep, so deep, under layers of delusion and arrogance that it might as well have lost all its flavor. He's often found young men to be that way, their trauma buried under so much denial that they didn't even realize they even had any. But they always make up for in raw sexual stamina.

It took Idlu a vast amount of energy to manifest into the quad, to bring even this old face forward, let alone his other form. And yet it was getting easier by the day. He knew why, of course; the skull, the games the students played with it. With each one of those little games, the aperture widened, letting him in. It would be so soon now that he could have his pick.

The two called Trey and Victoria he has not even had a passing taste of, and, yes, he would like to try them, too.

But as it stands, his number one choice, he thinks, as he runs through his options, is the one called Frankie.

Frankie, oh, she is delicious. He could feed off her alone for months. She's already provided him with such delicious sustenance and he's only just started. The absolute mountains of trauma that are packed inside that girl! The repression! Mwah!

Human religions were always good for providing him with that. Every single memory of Frankie Starling's childhood is so delicious and delectable, Idlu finds himself salivating at the mere thought. Oh, if only he could get inside her, he might accidentally gorge himself instantly, run her through and lick his fingers clean.

And he's so close now.

So close to being free to run this world.

Chapter 5

It shouldn't still look like that, Frankie thinks. It shouldn't still be warm, should it? She tells herself not to, but she can't help but look across the quad, to where the body of Zack Fort lays. Perhaps body isn't the right word, Frankie thinks. That implies a wholeness.

No, what's left of Zack is just blood. Just pieces. Do the police even think he's dead, or merely injured? Is what's left, the viscera that steams against the cold, the blood that coats the snow, enough to suggest death? Frankie remembers that monstrosity lifting bloody, red morsels up to its mouth. That's where Zack's gone. Inside something. Consumed by something. When they have his funeral, will they bury an empty casket?

"Ma'am?" A shape steps in front of Frankie, blocking her view of the bloody snow. She looks up, past what she slowly registers as a blue uniform, to a face.

A police officer.

Frankie has no idea how long he's been standing there trying to get her attention. He looks bored. Frankie can't stop looking at his hat. It's the fluffy kind with those little ear flaps. It makes him look like a little boy.

"Hello?" Frankie asks, confused why he's here, why he's talking to her. What is happening? What's she supposed to be doing? Something awful has happened, this she knows, but her brain is already hard at work cutting those memories away, sequestering them into a part of her mind she never intends to visit.

"Can you tell me what happened here?" the cop asks in the same unenthused way that someone would order a sandwich.

What did happen here? How would Frankie even begin to explain it? There was nothing she could say that would ever explain this adequately. But before she can even open her mouth, before she can even attempt to find a story, Vic is next to her.

"Nope!" she says, wrapping her arms around Frankie. "We request a lawyer present." She looks across the way, at Tanner and his friends, Delilah and Trey. Yes, there are other people with them, besides Frankie and Vic. It felt strange, in the aftermath of this violence, waiting for the police to arrive, doing introductions.

Nice to meet you, Trey.

At the very least, everyone else seemed as disconnected, as distant, as Frankie. Vic, her arms still around Frankie, removes one to point to the three of them. "Them too. Hey, Tanner!"

A few feet away, huddling against the cold in one of those aluminum foil-looking space blankets, Tanner jumps. He looks away from the police officer addressing him and over at Vic like she's just fired a shot. Delilah and Trey are huddled together under their own space blanket, lost in the quiet, looking everywhere except at the blood.

"What?" Tanner asks.

"Lawyer!" Vic calls, one hand over her mouth, projecting, the other arm wrapped tight around Frankie. "Do not say shit! Just say lawyer!"

That seems to dislodge something in Tanner, and some of the glassiness in his eyes falls away. He shuffles where he stands, like he can shake reason and logic back into himself, and then huddles deeper into the space blanket. He gently bumps Trey and Delilah, mumbles something to them. The cop speaking to the three of them deflates.

Frankie knows how this must make them look; three college students at the scene of something that looks very much like a murder, even with the lack of a body, all of them spattered with blood. None of them talking, all asking for lawyers. The look the cop standing next to her gives tells Frankie he doesn't see them as suspects, merely annoying, an unexpected hurdle that extended his shift, and it's in that look that her suspicions about police officers are confirmed.

Growing up, Frankie's mother always told her the police were her friends, that they were there to protect and serve, just like their badges said. Frankie guesses that still isn't entirely a lie; things would be different now if she—or any of them—were darker-skinned. As it stands, Frankie expects the cops to fight them on their lawyering-up, to act how police officers in the movies act; passionate about justice, about finding the criminal, the maniac still out there. But instead he looks like he's trying not to roll his eyes as he places his pen and paper back into his pocket.

The police officers get everything they need from the students; take their names, residences, student IDs numbers, and then tell them they'll need to talk as soon as possible—with their requested lawyers. They let them go and the three of them hurry away from the crime scene and the wet-copper smell of blood on snow.

Vic grabs Tanner by the arm while keeping her hold on Frankie.

"You're coming home with us," she says, pulling on him, dragging him back in the direction of their dorm tower. She looks at Delilah and Trey. "You two as well. We all need to talk."

The Fiona Lake Building is the Liberal Arts Center of Holstenwall College, one of the oldest buildings on campus, aside from the church and the original dormitories. A large, stone structure, in a similar Gothic design as the rest of the campus, it perfectly encourages young liberal arts majors to become nostalgic for a time of which they were never a part and that probably also didn't actually exist.

Vic picked it because it was the closest open building, but the fact that it has several wide common areas is a plus. She picks one with a large, stone mantle and fireplace that, for code reasons, no longer functions with wood and flame, but has been converted to electric. Tall, church-like windows loom above the fireplace, showing them the steadily-falling snow that, on any other occasion, they all might have found beautiful.

Vic, the only one who still has any of her wits about her, herds the group forward like a sheepdog. Delilah and Trey collapse onto the nearest couch, a wood-backed antique, while Tanner lists lazily in their direction, like he's drifting on an invisible current. Frankie slowly shuffles through the room, not doing anything, just standing. Vic looks around, down every available hall, but doesn't see any other students. When she's satisfied they're finally alone, she walks over to Frankie and helps guide her down onto the couch opposite Delilah and Trey.

Delilah laughs. It's a short bark, and she quickly covers her mouth with her hands, but when everyone looks at her, they see silent tears pouring out of her eyes.

Is this how it starts, she wonders, going crazy? She can't possibly have seen what her eyes told her she saw. It must be some sort of joke. Or an LSD flashback from that one time a couple years ago where she tried some at a frat party (not Alpha Chi). Or maybe there was some drug residue on the skull itself.

Tanner and Trey sidle closer to her, each putting their arms around her, taking her hands, pulling her up from the slippery slope of madness. She grips onto them tight, feeling their weight, grounding herself.

Both Vic and Frankie silently wonder which one is actually her boyfriend. It doesn't matter. There are more important things.

"Frankie, sweetie," Vic says, gently grabbing Frankie's face. "Look at me."

She does, but it's like she's high. Like she's in shock. This is what her mother expected. This is what she warned her about. She told Frankie about violence in the big cities, about the dangerous kinds of people that lived there. And though Frankie hasn't been victim to one of her mother's imagined stereotypes, she has been a victim to... something. Some monster. Maybe an actual demon.

Good Lord, her mother couldn't be right about that.

Could she?

"Frankie," Vic says, "was that the man from the party?"

But it's not Frankie who answers.

"Yeah," Tanner says from across the room. Vic looks up and at him. The glossiness, the shock, is gone from his face. He knows. He's damn sure. "That was him."

"And not just the party," Delilah adds. She laughs again with her mouth, but cries with her eyes. "I've..." But she doesn't finish. It sounds too preposterous.

"What?" Trey asks, gently nudging her.

"It can't be real," Delilah says.

Vic tells her, "I think we're past that now."

How is she so calm?

Delilah says, "I've seen him in my dreams."

Something dark settles over Tanner's face as he looks at Delilah and then over to Frankie. He doesn't need to say anything for Vic to know he's dreamed about this man too.

"What about you?" Vic asks Trey.

"Huh?" he asks, shellshocked.

"Have you seen that guy before?"

Trey shakes his head.

Vic does a quick mental calculation and realizes she and Trey are the only ones out of the group who have never played dominion.

Does that have anything to do with what's happening?

She's not sure yet, but it's something worth noting.

"Idlu."

Vic turns at Frankie's words.

"What?" Vic takes Frankie's hands in hers; it looks like she's coming back to herself.

"Idlu," Frankie says, but not entirely to Vic, more like through her, out into the room in the hopes that someone, anyone, would grab it. "That's his name. That's what he said. Joseph Idlu."

"Forget about his name," Trey says, some life coming back into him, "What about that thing? That fucking thing he turned into. What the fuck was that?" He can feel his voice growing out of control, more hysterical with each word. He holds on tight to Delilah to anchor him to the rational world.

"It was the skull," Frankie says. She blinks several times, finds she's actually looking across the room, actually making eye contact with people, coming back into herself. She looks at Delilah and then at Tanner. "You recognize it, right? The snout. The tusks. It had skin on it, but that's the skull we played dominion with."

"Yeah," Tanner says. "He talked about it before…" But he can't bring himself to say the rest.

The truth settles over the room. Or at least one angle of the truth. Frankie is right. They all recognize the shape of the head, that mouth full of tusks like a fistful of broken nails. There's a connection there, but they don't know what it is. They have two dots, but not yet a line to connect them. They're too far apart, nothing but an empty space in the middle.

Frankie looks at Vic, to see if she knows something, but she's on her phone.

"Victoria," Frankie says, almost heartbroken, wondering how she couldn't be paying attention at a time like this, but then she notices Vic's face, how pale it's gone, how wide her eyes are. Whatever Vic sees on that blue-lit screen, it's finally gotten her to break. "Victoria," Frankie says, slowly reaching out a hand. Vic realizes there's someone near to her and she suddenly pulls back, pulls the phone to her chest.

"What the fuck?" she says like Frankie's already seen, already knows, but Frankie reaches out and slowly takes the phone from her grasp. Vic doesn't resist. She turns the phone to face Frankie.

And shows her the face of Joseph Idlu.

"It's him," Vic says, turning her phone to face the rest of the group. "I Googled him."

Trey takes it from her shaking hand, reads the article headline; "Joseph Idlu, serial killer, executed."

And then he reads the date. Aloud. His voice shakes because none of this can be real. No, it can't be possible, but he nevertheless forces himself to say, for everyone else to hear, "March 4th, 1954."

They sit in silence for a long time, the rest of the article hanging in the air above them. Trey had started reading it aloud, and when he could no longer bring himself to continue, Delilah took over, narrating to the group the rampage of Joseph Idlu from decades ago. Delilah read everything with a distance that, quite frankly, alarmed her, considering the spots of blood of Idlu's latest victims on her jeans. Idly, she wondered if something inside her was broken for good.

She recited how Joseph Idlu seemed to be, by all accounts, an average, unsuspecting American. There was even a picture of him taken from his job at an early computing company where he looked wildly different; thick-framed glasses, clean-shaven face, short, black hair, gelled and side-parted. But then one day, the article said, he simply snapped, went on an indiscriminate murder spree across the American Southwest. He didn't have the patterns or M.O.s of a typical serial or spree killer, but seemed to take victims randomly, indiscriminately, using all manner of ways and weapons to kill all different kinds of people. There were reports of him cannibalizing some bodies, making strange art pieces out of others, spreading remains across state lines.

"This doesn't make sense," Delilah says, stopping in the middle of the article. "This is like how someone writes a serial killer in a movie. He's not sticking to one type of victim or weapon or method. No priors, no Macdonald triad."

Frankie doesn't know what that is, but she lets them continue.

"Then we're missing something," Tanner says.

But for all intents and purposes, the story of Joseph Idlu seems to end on March 4th, 1954, after being sentenced to death by electrocution after his arrest in Texas. Many of the articles went out of their way to mention the look of euphoria on Idlu's face as he was electrocuted.

"There's a bunch of mentions of Satanic shit," Delilah says, skimming that article and others, and eventually handing Vic's phone back to her.

Satanic shit, Frankie thinks, somehow still feeling the eyes of the crucified Christ still upon her. Could that be what they're dealing with? A devil? The devil?

"Plenty of homophobia when talking about his male victims and the...what he did to their bodies," Delilah continues, "But none of it looks like anything real. Just moral panic."

"So, how did we get from there to here?" Frankie asks, feeling a little more awake now that she has something to hold onto, a mystery to solve, even if it is a horrific one. "What about the skull? He wanted Zack to use the skull, right? That's what he was telling him, to keep using it."

"Yeah," Tanner says, "And he's showed up each time we used the skull."

"And," Delilah adds, "in dreams afterwards."

"And while we're awake," Frankie says, looking at her. Delilah returns a look that tells her she's sorry, both for forgetting, and because Frankie had to go through such a thing as the confessional booth.

Vic and Trey, the only two of them who haven't played dominion, look across the room at one another, but they each have nothing.

Trey says, "All this is only happening to people who have used it. Victoria and I haven't seen him before tonight."

Delilah nods. "The skull and Idlu are connected somehow," she says, "but how? Why would he want people to keep using it?"

"Each time we use it, he appears," Tanner says, more to himself than anyone else, adding another piece to their invisible puzzle.

"But there's also," Frankie says, slowly, not really wanting to bring it up, but knowing she has to, "that...thing. The monster that killed Zack and the others. That was the skull."

"With some skin on it," Tanner adds. "Whatever's going on, it's about that skull. So, what do we know about it?"

Frankie says, "All I ever heard was someone from the frat won it in a bet."

"But Idlu said Zack stole it," Trey says.

"I heard," Vic adds, "that a couple of the frat brothers found it in the desert."

Tanner says "Someone told me once they found it in an attic of the Epsilon house, like, decades ago."

"So, what we know is nothing," Delilah says flatly. "Urban legends and hearsay."

"What we know is the skull has something to do with it," Frankie says definitively, sitting up. "And we know where the skull is."

"Frankie, honey, what are you doing?" Vic asks.

"We need to get it," Frankie says, surprised at

the resolve in her voice. Where was this coming from? "We need to go get it now."

Everyone erupts in protest at once, their protesting voices crashing over one another.

"It's still at Alpha Chi Epsilon," Frankie says louder, ignoring each and every one of them, talking herself through the plan as she thinks of it. "That means the cops are going to find it soon. And take it. And then who knows what's gonna happen with it. We need to get it first."

"Whoa," Vic stands in front of her, holds her hands up, padding the air for Frankie to calm down. "Frankie, what the hell are you talking about?"

She can't explain it, doesn't know why, but retrieving that skull—destroying it—it's suddenly the most important thing in the world. It's not because of the world, though, because of the greater good. Yes, every time someone uses the skull, this Joseph Idlu appears. And, yes, every time he appears, bad things seem to happen. So, sure, the greater good is part of it, but it's not everything. Frankie just can't figure out what the rest is.

It reminds her of the feelings she couldn't entirely understand at the Epsilon house party. The feeling of being Delilah, of stepping into the center of so many eager hands and mouths and so many other parts that internalized shame can barely let her imagine. Enjoying the feeling of being wanted, but feeling a distant storm cloud looming over her, a cloud that slowly coalesced into the face of her mother, the face of her crucifix. But despite that looming, it was the first time in so long where she'd really felt free.

This feels like that.

Like if Frankie can destroy the skull, she can get out from under that storm cloud.

Holy shit.

Kyle can't believe it.

He's alive.

He's fucking alive.

Holy fucking shit, there's no way.

He shouldn't be alive. That giant thing that came for them? That fucking monster? He should be dead. As dead as...

Zack

Jesus.

He can hardly form the thought—it doesn't seem real but... Zack is... dead.

Kyle saw that beast—that monster...

He doesn't want to think about it.

He can't not think about it.

The horrific things he saw it doing to Zack's body.

Kyle can only think about the fact that he should be dead too, and though it feels like he's close, he's not.

He spends his first precious few moments of consciousness in a deep panic, looking at the blood coating him, coming from him, staining the snow around him. Screaming and moaning in the snow.

But after a moment, Kyle realizes the air feels cold around him because of the weather and not blood loss—even though he's lost some of that for sure—and he stops feeling scared and starts feeling mad.

Starts feeling fucking furious.

Starts feeling like he wants some payback.

With his good hand he pulls out his phone.

Chapter 6

When Frankie suggested destroying the skull, everyone protested the idea for different reasons, most of them concerning the imminent danger around the whole enterprise. Go in the direction of the thing that was in some way related to Zack Fort and Kyle Millner being ripped apart and eaten? They should be running as far away as possible.

But only Delilah knows Tanner's reason for protest is different. He can see it in her eyes as Frankie begins to rally the group to cross the campus again. Delilah knows because she knows what it was like to be him, that invisible tether connecting them as they shared flesh still somehow in place.

If the skull is destroyed, so is Tanner's way of feeling what he felt when he swapped bodies with Delilah.

"You okay?" Delilah asks him as Frankie leads the way back to the Epsilon house. No one liked the idea of anyone staying alone, so they all went together, hurrying across campus.

"I'm okay," Tanner says, lying. Obviously, he doesn't want to put anyone else in danger, but it all seems like it's moving too fast, Frankie pulling them all through the world in her determined wake. She leads them in a wide circle around the former-quad-now-crime-scene, very quickly filling up with campus security, actual cops, and EMTs. They'd cordoned off the whole area, so that all the students could see were swirling lights in the distance; red and blue splashing up the sides of the Gothic buildings, flashing out over the snow-covered ground. There were crowds now, of course, students looking down from windows or getting as close to the barrier as they dare.

"I want to feel it again too," Delilah says, quietly, so that only she and Tanner can hear. "But Frankie's right."

Tanner knows this, but that doesn't mean he can't feel bad about it.

They make it to the Epsilon house without incident, the huge, looming building with its Greek letters hanging above the door.

Frankie goes right in without knocking, surprised at her own brashness but not letting it slow her down. She guesses she's done a lot of things lately that the old Frankie never suspected she would have.

When you get to college, you keep those little legs of yours closed.

"Tanner, come with me," she says, feeling like a completely different person, "Everyone else, keep lookout."

They find the skull easily; it's hidden in the back of Zack's closet, behind an enormous, glass bong, a shoebox full of drug paraphernalia, assorted dirty clothes, and a stack of vintage Loveless porno magazines from the 80s.

Frankie pulls the velvet-swaddled package out carefully, unwrapping it only to check that it's correct, sure not to touch the bone itself with her bare hands. It reminds her of the dinosaur skulls she saw in books as a child. She looks at it with horror and revulsion. Tanner looks at it with a mix of fear and awe.

Let it go, he tells himself. This is bigger than you. There are other ways to feel how you want to feel. This is true, but there is nothing else that lets him feel the way he wants to feel so immediately.

"Jesus," Tanner whispers aloud, not thinking to apologize to Frankie like Vic does, but Frankie doesn't care anymore. There are more important things now. Looking down at the skull, she has the same feeling she did when she saw Idlu in the confessional. A sense of terror, a fear of not just death, but defilement. Being torn apart. Ravaged. She thinks about her mother, and thinks that if there is evil in the world, devils, like she says, this skull and the monster connected to it is the closest thing.

Tanner feels these things, the same horror Frankie feels, but he also sees a gateway, a portal. He can remember what it felt like to feel the denim of Delilah's jeans on him, the straps of her bra hugging his shoulders and his back, their comfortable bite into his skin.

"Tanner?" Frankie asks. He realizes she's looking at him quizzically. "You okay?"

"Yeah, I...Let's just get out of here." And he pushes those memories down.

"Okay," Frankie says as she and Tanner descend the stairs of the Epsilon house. "We've got it."

Trey says, "Then let's put an end to this

thing."

Without waiting for anyone else's approval, he snatches the backpack strap off Frankie's shoulder, whirls it around, up above his head, and slams it into the pavement at his feet. Everyone else jumps back at the sudden burst of violence, Tanner more than most. He's not ready for it to be here and now. He thought that maybe he had a couple more minutes to think of a plan, some sort of compromise.

But compromise how? He isn't even sure what he wants out of this situation.

Well, he knows what he wants, but he wants it without the demon.

Trey readjusts his grip, grabs both straps, and lifts the bag up again, slamming it up and down into the ground again and again. Tanner flinches hard with each strike, and he sees Delilah giving him a pitying look. She knows why he's hurting, and she comes over to him, puts her hand on his shoulder.

"I'm sorry," she whispers, low, so only he can hear. "After...let's talk? You and me?"

Tanner only nods, because it feels like if he says something, he'll hear his voice cracking.

But he realizes, past the sudden shock, that as Trey slams the bag down again and again, he doesn't hear any sound of shattering. None of them do. They watch as Trey leaves the bag on the ground and then stomps on it, but his foot easily glances off and he very nearly wipes out in the snow. He picks up the bag again, and this time with all his strength swings it into a nearby light pole. There's nothing but a loud, hollow gong as the bag ricochets uselessly off the metal.| "What the fuck?" Trey gasps, ripping open the zipper.

"Don't touch it!" Vic lifts her hands to her head, pulling at her hair.

"What?" Trey asks. "No one else is."

"We don't know if it'll, like, do anything else."

She has a point, and Trey is careful. He opens the bag, revealing the front of the skull, its toothy grin smiling up at them, nestled in its velvet pouch. A sudden and terrible pang of horror shoots through them all, except Tanner's is coated with a film of relief.

Maybe it doesn't have to be this way, he thinks. Maybe it doesn't have to end with destruction. Maybe he can still keep the skull, keep this experience. Somehow. His brain spins as he tries to think of a way.

"Not a goddamn scratch," Trey says, more to himself than anyone else.

"Let's get serious about this," Delilah says, reaching into her pocket. She pulls out a small ring of keys and twirls them around her finger. "Follow me."

She leads the group across the cold, dark campus to one of the parking garages and inside, her car; a big, ancient Ford pickup. Tanner tries to get her attention as they go, to exploit that tether between them, but she's just as determined to destroy the skull as the others.

"Keep it in the bag," she says to Trey as she hops into the cab. "Those teeth could pop a tire."

Trey lays the bag behind the right-rear wheel as Delilah starts the truck. Tanner looks at her, searching for... he doesn't know what, but when Delilah looks back at him, he can see it in her eyes too. Melancholy. She wants to keep it, not as much as he does, but he can tell she isn't finished exploring it.

Nevertheless, she backs over the skull.

Which does nothing. Delilah's huge truck is lifted up in the air like she's run over a curb. Tanner lets out the breath he's been holding.

"You've gotta be fucking kidding me," Vic sighs, leaning against the wall of the garage. "This isn't fucking real."

The group splits in two. Delilah and Frankie carry the bag to the top of the four-story garage and upturn the skull out of it, dropping it to the ground below, where Vic, Tanner, and Trey watch out for any pedestrians. It bounces off the cement, unharmed, and again Tanner feels relieved.

They find a quiet corner of campus between two largely-empty dormitories and douse everything in what remains of the vodka from Vic's room, setting it ablaze, but the only thing that burns is the backpack, the clothes, the velvet wrapping.

"What the fuck is it gonna take to kill this thing?" Delilah gasps. "Throw it into a goddamn volcano?"

Maybe now is the time, Tanner thinks to himself. If they can't destroy the skull, then they'll need to talk about where to put it for safekeeping. Who would be responsible for watching over it? A compromise. Yes, maybe he didn't have to interrupt anything at all. Maybe he didn't have to stop what was happening. Maybe he only had to guide the moment.

"Wait a minute," Frankie says. "What is that?" she asks, pointing.

Everyone looks down to the fire, to the flame-curled backpack. They don't see what she sees. Frankie walks over to a nearby tree and pulls a dead limb off, using it to push the smoldering pile around. Tanner and Delilah see it before Vic and Trey. Because they've seen the skull before. They've become intimately familiar with it.

And suddenly Tanner thinks, just like the others, despite what he still feels he knows about its powers, that keeping the skull is a terrible, awful idea.

Like she's disarming a bomb, Frankie gently

pushes one end of the crisping velvet away, revealing the entirety of the skull. Only it's not just a skull anymore.

It's a skull, with part of a spinal column attached to it.

"Oh, Jesus fucking Christ," Vic gasps, "It's growing."

She doesn't apologize for her blunder, and Frankie doesn't correct her.

It's impossible to think that what they see is anything else but what it is. It's not their minds playing tricks on them. They didn't somehow pick a different skull from the back of the closet. The one they have is undoubtedly, assuredly, growing. It has a spinal column now, yes, but also bits of skin clinging to the skull in random patches. Leathery and dried, but skin that still was not there before. It reminds Frankie of the sun-bleached animal skulls she'd see occasionally wandering the desert in Parthas. Despite lacking musculature or tendons or anything substantial, the spine still clings to the base of the skull.

"This didn't look like this before," Tanner says over and over again, in variation. "The other one was different." He tries to convince himself this is something else, anything else other than what reality tells him. He should not keep the skull, no matter what it makes him feel. Something evil is growing through it. And yet he still wants it.

"It wasn't another one," Delilah says, and she looks at Frankie to confirm her fears.

"It's the same skull," Frankie says, certain of it.

"Why?" Tanner asks. "How?"

Frankie thinks about Joseph Idlu telling Zack to use the skull again, egging him on to do it. Was that somehow adding skin to it, regenerating it?

She thinks about that shape of the dark.

"I don't care how," Frankie says, answering her own mental question out loud. She looks up at the others. "I don't care," she says again, shrugging. She can't get the thought of that enormous, flesh-completed monster out of her head. "I don't care why, I don't care how. All I know is he wants it, so we can't let him have it."

Tanner agrees with her, even though it feels like he's cutting a part of himself away to do it. He looks across the circle at Delilah, and she gives him the same look; I'm sorry. Maybe she's right. Maybe after this is over, they can figure something out together. People find ways to feel gender euphoria without the aid of a magic skull all the time, right?

"Well, what are we supposed to do?" Vic asks, gesturing down to the skull and its smoldering packaging. "We can't destroy it." They've tried bashing it, smashing it, running it over, setting it on fire. What's next, blowing it up? Someone mentioned a volcano earlier.

"What if we hide it?" Tanner asks, his tone much more thinking-out-loud than actual suggestion. It was one he'd thought of before; hide it, so he could secretly use it, but the thought of doing such a thing now seems dirty, and not in any kind of alluring way. "If we can't destroy it, maybe we bury it or something? Or, like, throw it in the ocean."

"How the hell are we gonna get to the ocean?" Trey asks.

"Someone else could still find it," Frankie says, determined. "No, we need this gone for good. Forever."

Trey gestures to the skull at their feet.

"We're open to suggestions."

But it's a new voice that answers her. A

familiar voice.

"My suggestion is that you step away from Alpha Chi Epsilon property."

They all turn to the nearby hedge where the voice came from, and see a hunched shape step out from behind it. He's silhouetted, dark against the lights from the campus walkway, holding his arms in on himself.

"Kyle?" Frankie gasps.

"Oh, shit," Tanner breathes, "you're alive? We thought you..." but he can read the moment. They all can. And it's not one of relief. Kyle isn't there to help. He's holding his left arm tight to his body, a look of rage on his face.

"Step away," Kyle practically growls, "from the skull."

And as he does, half a dozen more tall, strong silhouettes join him.

The Alpha Chi Epsilon brothers, boxing them in.

Chapter 7

*T*he gang *of Epsilon brothers* bring them back to the library. The Robert Mayer Library, where just days ago all of this started. Sure, everything had happened at the Epsilon house, but things had roiled inside Frankie since then, grown and metastasized, and she'd felt different when she was on the roof. She'd reached an inflection point. And taking one path over the other had brought her here. Maybe, even though she didn't realize it at the time, both paths end in the same place. She guesses all paths do, if you walk them long enough.

The front door to the library was unlocked, and Frankie wasn't sure if it was meant to actually be open to students during this time, or if it was the kindness of librarians, or the hubris of the affluent, to think that no one would want to break into a library. Either way, the place was empty, and the frat brothers led the kids in through the front doors and down into the basement, since we can't go home, Kyle said.

Each of them were made to sit in chairs, surrounded by the Epsilon brothers in a small clearing amongst the library's shelves of old, dusty, uncatalogued material, fluorescent lights glaring above them. One of the brothers placed the skull reverently upon a nearby table, its eyeless sockets glaring out.

"What the fuck happened out there?" Kyle growls, looking out over the captured group. He's told his brothers the bare minimum, because it's all he understands. Something happened with that old man and Zack was killed. That thing, it fucking... it ate him. "What did you do?"

When he asks this, he looks directly at Frankie, holding his injured arm to his chest. It's wrapped hastily in a sweatshirt that's already soaked through with his blood, drip-drip-dripping onto the tile floor.

"We didn't do shit," Vic growls, but lowers her voice when she feels two of the Epsilon brothers close in on either side of her.

"You've got to destroy it," Frankie says, looking past Kyle, past his pointed accusation, to the skull on the table. She can feel the hollows of its eyes. "It's... connected to a monster or something, I don't know. But that's what killed Zack."

"A monster?" he asks, like he's expected to believe that. He saw something, but he doesn't know what it was. It could have been a hallucination for all he knew. He probably still had some drugs of some kind in his system.

"You fucking saw it, Kyle!" Tanner shouts. Several of the Epsilon brothers shoot glances over at Kyle. All they knew when he came rushing in was that Zack was hurt, maybe dead, and that he needed backup for the fuckers who'd not only done it, but stolen their skull.

"I didn't see shit," Kyle says. "I saw you five fuckers," he points at them all, "and that old man. Now who is he? Where is he?"

"Kyle," Frankie says, drawing his eyes to her, "look at the skull. Does it look like your skull?"

Kyle doesn't move, but several of the brothers do, their eyes going wide as they finally take in the differences—the additions; the patches of skin, the goddamn spinal column.

"Yo, man, she's right," one of them says, "There's something up here." He breaks away from the circle and takes a better look at it.

"Don't get distracted," Kyle says, waving his good hand, not taking his eyes off the group, off Frankie. This night was supposed to be going so differently. He was supposed to be getting laid right now, maybe even by Frankie if he'd been lucky enough. But even more of his brothers take their eyes off the prize, turning to look at the skull. "Oh my god, what?" Kyle turns around and looks at it, and finally sees they're right. He sees the spinal column, the skin, little patches of hair.

He wheels on the group.

"What did you do?" he barks.

"Not us," Frankie says, more calmly than she expects. "It's him. The old man. He is the skull. The more you use it, the more it's gonna grow, and then that monster is gonna come back."

Vic says, "You have to destroy it or what happened to Zack is gonna happen to a lot more people."

"Destroy it?" Kyle chuckles. "Do you have any idea what this thing can do?" He turns around and picks the skull up off the table, brings it over to them. He looks at his brothers, "Grab their hands."

The Epsilon brothers close in on the

students, thick arms and fingers closing around each one of them, holding them still as Kyle approaches with the skull.

"Tanner Little," he says, sidling up to him first. The Epsilon brothers holding Tanner keep him rooted to the seat, pull his arm out by the wrist, make him reach for the approaching skull. "I know you of all people don't wanna get rid of this," he says, lifting the skull to Tanner's hand, "because I saw what you did the other night."

Tanner tries to pull away, but the Epsilon brothers are too strong, and when he feels the warm bone under his fingertips —Jesus fuck, why is it warm? – he feels what it was like to be Delilah again. A soft warmth wrapping itself around him like a blanket. A power, an energy, he could almost reach out and grab it.

"You feel that, don't you?" Kyle asks, looking at Tanner. "Why the hell would I ever wanna give that feeling up? Why would you when it could give you what you want?"

Kyle pulls the skull away from Tanner and brings it over to Frankie, makes her touch it. She, too, feels that warmth, like the first toe-dip into a hot bath, except a thousand times more pleasurable. Not just sexually, but physically. She feels it all over, and she can feel the echoes of what she felt that night too. She doesn't think of her mother or of growing up in Parthas, doesn't think of that empty desert and those rules that chained her down. All she thinks about is the pleasure of the flesh. Not just the pleasure from flesh, but the pleasure of flesh. She remembers the night at the Epsilon house, but she also remembers the breakfast Vic brought her and can taste the bacon again on her tongue. She can feel Vic's arms around her, holding her, comforting her, the warmth of her body. She can feel the bite of snow on her fingertips and the taste of orange juice, and finds herself reaching after the skull as Kyle pulls it away.

"No," Frankie pants just as hard as she did that night, glaring at Kyle, "bring it back." She looks over at her friends and realizes what she's done, how they see her, and she tries to compose herself.

"Don't you want to keep feeling that way?" Kyle asks. He goes down the line of students, touching the skull to each of them, and they are all taken over by a similar euphoric feeling. Nerves and sensations turned up to eleven, each of them remembering all the pleasures they've felt over the past weeks, reliving recent memories, and each of them moaning in similar anguish when the skull is pulled away.

"Jesus Christ, what the fuck was that?" Vic pants, the last one to experience the sensations of the skull.

"Feels good, doesn't it?" Kyle asks.

Vic looks down the line at the others.

"That's what you've been doing?" she's breathing hard, hair clinging to her sweaty forehead. She huffs, shrugs. "I think I get it now."

"That's not even the best part," Kyle says. "We're gonna play a little game now. But we're going to add a wrinkle. Let's call this version roulette." He grabs a small desk/chair and drags it into the middle of the room, dropping the skull down onto it. It's grown yet again. Not just skin now, but muscles and hair. It's beginning to look like something that has only recently died, rotted, but not yet even picked at by scavengers. "Everybody's gonna put their hands in. And then you switch."

"No, man," Trey shakes his head. "I don't wanna do this." But two Epsilon brothers, the biggest of them, are holding him tight.

"Tough shit," Kyle says.

"Why are you doing this?" Frankie gasps as one of the brothers pushes her chair closer to the skull. It's looking at her. He grabs her hand, just like all the other brothers grab her friends, placing their hands on the bone. "You've got the skull, that's what you want, isn't it?"

Kyle smiles, and it's far too similar to Idlu's.

"This is what I want."

Frankie had only ever swapped one at a time. Tanner and Delilah were the same, playing lightheartedly, simple one-on-one swaps, the sensation a brief tugging behind the bellybutton, a drunken sway before arriving at your new, temporary destination.

None of them had ever done anything like this.

Where the one-on-one swap was a quick jolt before reorientation, this is like being dragged through the mud from the back of a car, your destination unknown, senses overwhelmed. They—yes, all of them existing as one, because no one is sure of who is who anymore—are able to pick out certain images and feelings. Somewhere beyond their bodies, and yet still inexplicably connected to them, they slam together and rip apart, no longer individuals but mashing together like humans made of slime, skin and bone blended into one gelatinous, fleshy monstrosity. Trey's teeth are in Frankie's mouth and Delilah's hands are at the end of Vic's arms and Tanner sees a dick that cannot be his own growing out of his crotch and Frankie feels her chest shrink from breasts to pectorals and expand back again past their normal size and they all mash together like one terrible, nuked Guernica.

It's those nights at Alpha Chi Epsilon all over again, and everyone can feel what it was like to be Frankie looking back at herself, at Delilah, who stood on the sidelines, said she just wanted to watch, that Frankie should go ahead, have fun, let loose, and before she knew what she was doing she was in the middle of the morass herself, peeling her clothes off, not feeling the shame she felt had her own body been nude. Because she wasn't her. So this didn't count. Which both made sense and didn't. Frankie wanted to know what it felt like and so she grabbed the first person she could and pulled his face to hers. She felt his lips, his tongue, felt his hard, throbbing penis pressing against her hip as he turned towards her, and before she knew it she was on her back, hands and mouth everywhere, reaching, feeling, determined to consume every bit of pleasurable flesh she could. She stuck her fingers into a sopping wet hole she found only by touch. She let someone guide her borrowed hand to a throbbing cock and she worked it, pulling it to her mouth nervously, and then excitedly, hungrily. She cried out in pain and then as pleasure as something that could only have been a penis found its way inside her and hands gripped her hips, holding her tight.

I'm still a virgin, she thought, because such a thing had been important to her then, because she couldn't undo a lifetime of conditioning with all the pleasure in the world. At least not right away. She thought it would be different, that she would feel vulnerable, but instead she felt powerful, more powerful than she ever had in her life, like all these guys were lining up to worship at the altar of her. And when she finally crested the plateau of her own orgasm, brought on by a freckled redhead's mouth between her thighs, she screamed like everything in her world was being ripped apart. Because it was.

Because she could never go back to the way things were because of what she'd learned there that night.

Why had she waited this long? This was what bodies could do, she wondered? This was what she had been missing out on? Such dizzying, terrifying heights had been kept from her? Why had she waited this long?

Except it doesn't stop.

Kyle says the words again and before any of them can understand who they're inside they're moving again. Each time they think they're about to get settled, Kyle bounces them around the ring of bodies. Pain and pleasure become intermingled, confused, and everything that is supposed to hurt becomes delicious and everything that is supposed to feel good hurts. Nothing means anything anymore, or maybe it means everything, or maybe everything at once simply creates a numbness, all of them enthralled and also repulsed, begging for it to stop like they're at the mercy of one continually-forced orgasm after another.

But Kyle just keeps saying the words. He says them like a chant, zapping their souls across the ring of bodies over and over again, and Frankie—it might be Frankie but it might not because no one knows who anyone else anymore outside of the whole— either pees someone's pants or comes in them and she—he, they, maybe—cannot tell which.

Beyond them, the skull steadily regrows skin and muscle. Exaggerated eyes pop into its sockets, bursting cartoonishly large before shrinking back down to size, and each one of the students fears the darker-than-dark shadow that killed Zack, clawing its way to reality.

The Epsilon brothers, Kyle included, release their captives and scatter back against desks and chairs and bookshelves.

The heinous skull has become a skeleton, the horrible reality of the muscle and flesh of that dark thing that's Joseph Idlu's true face. It stitches itself together, mouth wide, tongue lolling, head thrown back in atavistic pleasure and he's here, there, in the world with everyone else.

The game stops.

Idlu's sneering maw turns directly to Kyle.

You've been a good boy, Idlu says, somehow aloud, despite the fact that this true mouth is incapable of human speech.

"Wait, wait!" Kyle gasps, "No, I'm not—"

Idlu grabs him by the shoulders, those eagle-like talons so large they wrap around him entirely, jagged nails the size of railroad spikes biting into his chest and back. Kyle screeches, high-pitched and awful, and the monster opens his jaw wide and bites down, silencing him.

Frankie, head still swimming from jumping body to body to body, lies there on the floor like she's drunk, unable to move. Vic is lying directly in front of her, screaming something as she stumbles to her feet, but Frankie can't hear her over the rush of blood in her head, the screams of the Epsilon brothers. Some of them scatter, some of them pick up chairs and tables, throwing them at the monstrous shape that's clawed its way into the world, the shape that's ripping holes in their frat brother.

Frankie looks down at herself and breathes a sigh of relief; she's in her own body. Quick as she can, she gets her own feet under her.

It's been so long. He has no idea how long. So long

since he's felt, really felt, the taste of blood on his lips. So long since he's felt the weight of his muscles, the ground under his feet. Fuck, even blunt smack of chairs and the stab of scissors from those boys feel pleasurable. Tiny little penetrations that do no more to him than insect bites.

Idlu pulls his hands apart and tears the little flesh-thing that calls itself Kyle in two. He feels the weight of blood and meat slide down his throat and the tear of the tiny body in his talons, the spray of blood across his front as he rips him asunder.

Heavenly.

He falls upon the others like a predator, his tusked snout ripping into someone's stomach, perforating guts, and he can smell—gods, he can finally smell again—half-digested hamburger and shit. The screams stop but that's okay because his own wails of earthly, carnal pleasure continue.

The students are up and running, headed up the stairs and towards the library's main exit, but a couple of them are running strangely. Frankie's in the lead, and when she looks back over her shoulder she sees Tanner and Delilah tripping over themselves, and she knows it's because they're not Tanner and Delilah. They're one another.

Another problem, but she doesn't know the solution.

She'll figure it out later.

If they survive.

Vic is running like herself, but Trey isn't running at all, standing at the base of the stairs, looking back into the carnage in the basement.

"Trey!" Frankie shouts, and it feels like it tears her throat apart. Like she's going to be sick. "Come on!"

Trey looks back up at her, and Frankie sees something in his eyes. An unexpected sorrow that curls into a scowl of rage.

Because it's Kyle looking back at her through those eyes.

It wasn't supposed to happen like this. Oh, Jesus, Jesus fuck, this wasn't supposed to happen! This was just supposed to be a game! He just wanted to have a little fun before he took the skull back, before he let them go. He was gonna let them go! But now that fucking monstrosity's ripping his brothers apart.

"Trey!" Frankie shouts from above him. "Come on!"

Kyle looks up at her through eyes that aren't his own.

This all started with her.

It's her fault.

Frankie Starling is going to fucking pay.

Frankie kicks open the door to the first floor and props it open but doesn't take it, instead grabbing a fire extinguisher off the wall and pulling the pin. She reaches for Delilah's ponytail and yanks out her hair-tie, wrapping it around the extinguisher's nozzle and hurling it down the stairs at Kyle-in-Trey's-body.

"What are you doing?" Delilah screams as Tanner, unable to hold herself upright. The foaming extinguisher clogs up the stairwell, and Kyle lifts his shirt to cover his face as he's lost in a cloud of mist.

"That's not Trey," Frankie growls, grabbing both Delilah and Tanner and pushing them up the stairs.

Behind her, Vic says, "Then Trey..." but

doesn't finish. Frankie looks over her shoulder and scowls at Vic.

"Help me!" she shouts, pushing her staggering friends up the stairs. Vic bites down on whatever she was going to say and follows, triggering the fire alarm on the way.

Stupid bitch thinks she's clever, Kyle thinks, looking at the propped-open door to the first floor. His borrowed ears are ringing, but they're still good enough to tell him there's movement above.

He follows.

Frankie and Vic push the staggering Delilah and Tanner up onto the roof. A rush of feelings she can't afford to feel come back to her, and she bites them all down as she shoves the group out into the snow. She can hear Trey's stolen body right behind them, not fooled by her ruse, and then behind that, something huge.

Something terrifying.

Idlu.

Frankie turns around and tries to shut the door to the roof, but Kyle is already there. Part of her wants to hesitate because she sees Trey, but she tells herself that's not who this is, that's not what this is, and slams the door, but Trey is bigger, he's so much bigger, and he shoulders the so hard he knocks Frankie off her feet, sending her skidding into the snow.

"Trey?" Delilah steps forward in Tanner's body, and there's a hesitation on both their parts.

It's just enough.

It's too much.

They're less than two feet apart when the first talon goes through Kyle—through Trey's chest—and into Delilah's. Tanner, in a borrowed body, watches in horror as his own is run completely through, pierced and joined together with Trey's as if they're some sort of human shishkabob. The powerful hand attached to the talon lifts them off their feet, this grotesque parody of lovers, and holds them aloft.

The Idlu-thing pulls its talons to its face so it can lick the blood running off its forearm, and then it flicks its wrist, sending Delilah and Kyle flying away. They crack into the wall with a sickening dry noise and slump to a tangled mess on the floor.

Oh, the thing moans, lifting its arms to the sky, speaking to them in its soundless way. Oh, you've no idea how good it feels to be outside again. How good it feels to feel.

It lowers its head and stares out across the roof, eyes glancing over Vic and Tanner (inhabiting Delilah), and then to Frankie.

Oh, Frankie, it shudders, stepping closer, you have no idea how good you're going to feel. It's gonna be the fuck of your life.

"Then come get me," she says in a bedroom purr.

Idlu charges, slobbering, blinded by desire, by his need, thinking of everything he'll do not just to her, but to them all, to the world, now that he's free. He runs forward, skidding in the snow, his talons out and grasping, and Frankie's arms are open wide, welcoming him, beckoning him, and he's too blinded to see. The tumble.

The fall.

So, this is what the view would have been like. Staring up from the brick walkway in front of the library.

It's not so bad now, Frankie thinks, looking up into the steadily falling snow. It wasn't enough to kill her. Not that she thinks that's what she wanted anymore. Not really. Everything hurts and everything's cold and everything's wet and she doesn't think she can feel anything in her body anymore.

But somehow she turns her head, or maybe her head simply turns, pulled by gravity, and she can see the enormous Idlu-thing lying next to her, bifurcated completely by the knight statue that stands guard before the library. The way they're lying together, it's almost like they're lovers, each lying on their own snowy pillow, looking up into the night. She can feel what Idlu feels, and to him that's what it's like.

A great fuck.

The last fuck, pain and pleasure indistinguishable for him now, as she finally sees the steam of his breath, and it stops coming and his eyes empty out into nothing.

Frankie watches his horrid mouth for a long time, making sure he doesn't take a single breath more, and then she passes out.

Chapter 8

O*nce again, Frankie sees* Holstenwall's old stone buildings, its snow-covered campus, painted with the reds and blues of police and EMT lights. Only this time, instead of running away, she's the one at the center of it all. Vic is above her, and Frankie can feel, somewhere far, far away, Vic's hands holding hers. Vic's telling her she needs to stay awake, that she whatever she does, she can't pass out because isn't that what people are supposed to say, but Frankie's so cold and so fucking exhausted and when uniformed figures loom above her, pushing Vic out of the way, everything around her is suddenly warm and that exhaustion finally takes her.

The EMT shuts the back door of the ambulance, pounds on it with her closed fist. It takes off into the night, the three surviving girls inside, swirling lights painting the campus a bloody red. A different vehicle will be coming to collect the corpses. Corpses could wait.

The EMT breathes out a plume of steam, watching the ambulance go, watching the spot where it disappeared even after it's gone because as long as she looks at that, she doesn't have to turn around and look at what remains, speared across the statue in front of the library, splattered across the entryway and over the front doors.

The body of that...

Thing.

She has no idea what it is, how to even begin to describe it. It looks like a mutant bear or something. A bear in New England. Not impossible. But a bear that fell off the roof of a college library after killing a group of students in the basement and then chasing others up four flights of stairs?

Still, she stays away from the impossible thing, joins her fellow EMTs inside attending to the other corpses while the cops keep a perimeter outside, because attending to corpses still sounds more appetizing than waiting outside until animal control comes to check on whatever the hell this thing is.

Because she swears she can feel that thing's dead eyes staring up at her.

When Frankie wakes up, there's a heavy pressure on her left side, and when she shifts herself even slightly, she hears, "Holy shit, you're alive!" The pressure moves, adjusts itself onto her chest, and immediately evaporates when she winces. "Shit, shit, sorry! For the cursing and for squishing you."

Frankie blinks her vision clear and finds Vic sitting on her bed next to her. She's beaten and bruised, but her wounds have been tended to; stitches, gauze, tape, maybe some painkillers, judging by the struggling-to-focus look in her eyes. Frankie knows the same thing must have happened to her. She looks down, taking stock of the damage, and sees very much the same, with one major addition; her leg is in a cast.

"I can't...feel it," she says slowly, slurring her words, panic rising in her stomach. Why can't she feel it?

Vic touches the tip of Frankie's exposed toe with finger.

She feels it. Thank Christ, she feels it.

"It's the drugs," Vic says. "Broken tibia, they said. In addition to," she waves her hand in Frankie's general direction, indicating her bumps and bruises, cuts and stitches.

"Did they call my mother?" Frankie asks.

"We're not kids anymore," Vic says, and Frankie lets out a breath she didn't realize she was holding. She would have to tell her eventually, but at least her walking through the door wasn't an immediate concern.

"So, it's over?"

Vic nods.

"It's over. The cops took Idlu's body. They're cremating it."

"Delilah?" Frankie asks.

At that, Vic takes a long, deep breath.

Tanner is not Tanner.

He's closer to what he should be, he can feel it. But it shouldn't have happened like this. He swings his borrowed legs out of bed and hobbles into the hospital bathroom, feeling the pain in his borrowed body every step of the way.

When he turns the light on, a battered, bruised, stitched-up Delilah Morse looks back at him from the mirror.

A gasp escapes their lips, and then a cry, and then they turn the light off because they can't stand to look at what they've become.

What they feel like they've stolen.

Because it is they now, isn't it? Even though Tanner is in there alone—Delilah left in his old body, run through by Idlu—he has crossed a border. Tanner is no longer he, but they, something different, someone different, even before this terrible, accidental swap. The possibility he'd bumped up against when he first played dominion is now their reality.

Tanner can feel their braless breasts hanging a little lower onto their stomach, feel the weight of more fat stored around their hips, in their upper arms, in the bottom of their tummy, and it feels right, feels like it should, but they hate how they've come to it.

They throw their hands over their mouth to stifle a cry and wander out of the bathroom, but while there is escaping the sight, there is no escaping the feeling. It follows them wherever they go, feeling right, but at a cost they'd never even begun to imagine.

Tanner flops down onto the hospital bed, looks at the small pile of Delilah's clothes sitting in the chair next to the bed.

Is it still there, they wonder?

Tanner grabs the jacket and lifts it up, digs into the inside pocket. Finds it.

The thing they'd held onto desperately as the paramedics had looked them over in the aftermath of what happened in the library. The thing they'd quickly hidden, desperate for them to not find it, though not knowing why. It's still warm to the touch, like it's alive.

A long, sharp, canine tooth.

It's in several large, red biohazard trash bags. The body of the thing they're saying killed all those kids at the college upstate. Taking all those bags down into the basement of the crematorium is not a two-man job because the bags are particularly heavy. Or because there are so many of them. But because they're frightened. The cops said it was a rabid bear. The news said it was a rabid bear. But Tom and Greg have been to zoos. Hell, they've got the internet. They look up pictures of bears on their phones.

They've never seen any bears that look like what's in those trash bags.

They weren't supposed to, said the federal guys who dropped the remains off to be disposed of, but they cut a slit in one of the bags with a pocketknife, and the decapitated head that looks back up at them looks like some unholy combination of a bear and a boar. Something out of nightmares with a mouth full of tusks and razor-sharp teeth, eyes that are supposed to be dead, but nevertheless seemed to stare right up at the both of them with a hungry glee.

They immediately put the head back into another bag. And throw that bag, along with all the others, into the oven, turning it on full blast, higher than they really ought to, and wait, standing as far as they can across the room, trying to ignore the rushing flames that sound so much like an animal roaring.

THE END

Acknowledgements

Tons of people helped with the creation of this book, whether in actually working on it or helping me get through it. First and foremost, Chris ! and Phi of Little Ghosts who took a chance on one of the more bizarre things I've written, for absolutely crushing the edits to prepare for StokerCon, and for believing in stories like this in a time when people want to see our voices smothered.

Thank you to the Weirdos in the Wild, my Horror Writer Group, and the GTTUnit for living in my phone and being constant sources of camaraderie, and Will and Kristen of *Guide to the Unknown* for providing an endless spooky playlist of things to explore for inspiration.

A huge thanks to my wife for far too many things to list on an acknowledgements page, and to my family who dips their toes into horror because it's a thing I like, I'm sorry for what you just read.

TT Madden (they/them) is a Pushcart-nominated, genderfluid, mixed-race writer who refuses to keep "politics" out of their writing. They've written in the sandboxes of big IPs, helping create the *Blair Witch* and *Agatha Christie* tabletop mystery games for Hunt a Killer, but they much prefer writing smaller, weirder stories that make you uncomfortable, but in a way you hopefully want to explore more. Their short prose has been published by Ghoulish Tales, Bag of Bones Press, and Speculation Publications, among others. They can be found at ttmaddenwrites.carrd.co when they're not wandering the woods around their home, looking for spooky inspiration.

Also by T.T. Madden...

Available now:

The Familialists
The Cosmic Color

Forthcoming:

2025

Gorman's House
places where you cannot be: an afro-american travel guide
The Neon Revelation

2026

The Shapes of Our Screams
The Familialists second edition
No Chains Will Ever Hold Us: Tales of Identity Horror
Dream of the Machine Child (working title)

About Little Ghosts Books

Little Ghosts Books is a horror bookstore and small press established in Toronto, Canada in 2022, with a vision to showcase indie horror from diverse voices.

Through our publishing imprint and physical space, we hope to connect readers, horror lovers, authors, and folks of all backgrounds.

Find out what we already know:
A Good Story Will Haunt You.

FOLLOW LITTLE GHOSTS:
@littleghostsbooks
www.littleghostsbooks.com

9 781738 909797